The Golden Dog

Scott Sipprelle

For more information about this novel please visit:
www.TheGoldenDogNovel.com

Printed in the United States of America

ISBN: 1-4392-4081-7
ISBN-13: 9781439240816
LCCN: 2009904612

FOR TRACY, NURTURER OF MY DREAMS

CHAPTER ONE

The peninsula that constitutes Long Island, stretching out to sea like a slender finger, has always beckoned mariners toward the calm asylum of New York's upper bay, where the lower edge of the island of Manhattan sits calmed between the heights of Brooklyn and the flats of New Jersey. But the development of Manhattan as a crossroads of commerce and conspiracy cannot be explained merely by geography.

When the three masts of Henry Hudson's ship, sailing for the Dutch East India Company, passed through the narrows between present-day Staten Island and Brooklyn in 1609, the Indians who hunted her fields and fished her shores marveled at the arrival of what they believed were god-like white men in a floating house. The awed natives welcomed Hudson's entourage enthusiastically, offering a sumptuous feast of their finest delicacies as well as abundant supplies of tobacco leaves, which they taught the sojourners how to smoke out of carved bowls.

Hudson and his men reciprocated the gestures of goodwill, bartering knives and other useful objects with the wondrous qualities of metal in exchange for the tobacco and other essential foodstuffs. The Europeans also introduced their hosts to the pleasures of alcohol. The native word Manahachtanienk, *meaning "place of inebriation," provided both a name for this early Dutch settlement and also a motif for Manhattan's ensuing commercial expansion.*

⁓

Not too long after I got my first job on Wall Street, the stock market crashed. It was 1987 and I had been working at Platt Brothers, one of the Street's leading firms, for only two months when the storm hit. The financial press wailed about the worst percentage decline in stock prices since the Great Depression while the cranks warned of a doomsday alignment of the planets. But out on the streets, the cabbies and the food-cart vendors went boisterously about their daily routine.

When I look back, that day was a sure signal that something disruptive lurked in the eastern city of my dreams. As I had only recently moved to New York, I felt like the perplexed tourist who enters one subway station in full daylight, only to emerge at the end of his trip into a sudden hailstorm.

My decision to move to New York and enter the financial services business—as it liked to call itself, but which others just thought of as "the stock market"—was an act of arrogance in the first place. I was a kid from a straight-bordered state in the middle of the country, armed principally with the encouragement of a man named Wertz, calling on the gilded halls of high finance with high hopes and trepidation.

The ambition I carried with me to New York could be traced back to a confidence instilled by "Bull" Wertz, my high school physics teacher and the best instructor I ever had. To walk into Bull Wertz's classroom was to enter nature's workshop. He dispensed with textbooks, theory, and any pretense of grand tutorial and instead molded his students with lessons learned through real life experience. On the first day of class, before he even began to speak, Wertz introduced Newton's first law of motion by grabbing an apple from his desk, and whipping it toward the back row, where I sat. I caught the apple.

"An object at rest will stay at rest, and an object in motion will stay in motion at constant velocity unless acted upon by an unbalanced force. You there—in the back row—you represent the unbalanced force."

If I had chosen to sit in the front of Wertz's classroom that day, his projectile would not have ended up clutched in my palm. I would not have stopped by after class to return the fruit, and I would not have engaged in the simple banter that began our relationship. Instead, we became friends. Over casual conversations, I soon discovered that my unassuming teacher was mesmerized not so much by the subject he taught as by the faraway world of Wall Street. I suppose I was struck by the contradiction. While he revealed the steady discipline of applied science day after day as he appeared in front of the class wearing his rotation of rumpled, short-sleeved shirts, Bull Wertz was fascinated by the universe of speculative pursuits and pinstripe suits.

I was a good enough student, particularly good at memorizing things, but until I got to know Wertz, my attitude toward life and my own future had been one of a bland lack of curiosity. I suppose I was expected to follow my father into business. Dad ran the auction sales department for a farm equipment company that operated in three states, and he made a good living bringing verve to the resale of tractors and backhoes. Most of my classmates would likely head off to community college before landing dead-end local service jobs. Neither option excited me. Wertz was my escape, and under his influence, I became a refugee from the routine and expectations of my family and friends. I began to share his fascination with high finance, and the stock market in particular.

Wertz was consumed by Wall Street and well studied in its lore. When he had concluded that I was to become his disciple, he showered me with his knowledge, particularly the teachings of Ben Graham. Graham was the father of twentieth century security analysis, a man who taught his legions of followers that an intelligent investor could outwit the market. In Graham's view, the stock market was like a moody door-to-door salesman, offering prices that often reflected emotion and personal circumstance more than intrinsic value. "Wait for the seller's desperation," Wertz would say, reflecting Graham's philosophy.

When I went away to state university, Wertz and I stayed in touch. From time to time he would write me letters describing his latest investment skirmishes with "Mr. Market," including extensive details about his most recent stock purchase and the rationale behind his decision. Over Thanksgiving of my senior year, when I came home on vacation, I stopped by my old classroom to tell him that I had decided to apply to Columbia University's Graduate School of Business, the very institution where Graham had once held court.

Columbia accepted me, and for two years I studied at the grand old campus on Morningside Heights in Manhattan. I drifted away from Wertz, but as I pursued my finance studies in his mecca, I still felt like a kid from Kansas, countrified and callow. It was as though I had arrived for a theatrical production well after the curtain had gone up. Even with my ticket in my hand—two years at Columbia and a pretty good transcript—I felt as though I was wandering bewildered through the aisles of a darkened arena, trying not to bump into obstructions as I went.

Despite my lack of confidence, I was hired by Platt Brothers, one of Wall Street's most venerable investment banks. At the time I wondered if they were intrigued by the fact I was from Kansas. Perhaps they thought I represented old-fashioned Midwestern values and decency. Later I discovered that my position had opened up when another candidate had pulled out of the running. Unlike most of my B-school peers, I did not wait around to deliberate between competing proposals. I remembered what my dad had said when the people next door put their house on the market, waited too long to get the asking price, and got considerably less. "The first offer is usually the best offer."

I entered the training program as one of twenty. Beginners were put through a rotation, during which the heads of each division addressed the rookie class of newly hired hopefuls, sniffing out talent and attempting to make his (or, very occasionally, her) department sound like the most exciting and profitable place to work. Sometimes one of us caught the attention of a managing director and got invited to join his department. At first I was offered a position in research, reflecting, I suppose, a belief that I had exhibited the requisite qualities of curiosity and thoroughness. But I deflected this advance. Research wasn't the Wall Street that Wertz and I had visualized. I wanted to be where the action was, not tethered to a world of spreadsheets and late nights in the office. I also needed the time and freedom to explore my new world.

I ended up in the institutional stock department, indentured to work alongside a veteran broker named Doug Talley, a man who wore his spit-polished shoeshine like an act of professional hygiene. Talley was the first exhibit I encountered in the museum of deception. On Wall Street, things were not always as they appeared.

My business school experience and expectations had not exactly prepared me for my meager starting role at Platt Brothers. I answered the phone when Talley was busy on another call, I fetched reports from the research department to send out to clients, I sat obediently and silently in meetings, and I took orders for the afternoon coffee run at two thirty. I had the impression that Talley found me more an annoyance than a useful aide. He was so dismissive that he usually communicated by handing over a scribbled note without looking at me.

When it came to the rest of the room, Talley knew how to play to the crowd. If a major client called, he would stand up, cup his ear, as though to be sure he heard correctly, and shout to his secretary, "Who is it?"

Her role was to shout back the name loudly enough so it could be heard all along the open rows of connected desks where the salesmen sat. After he was certain that everyone within earshot was alerted, he would bellow, "Hey, Lee!"—or whomever—into the phone, and then he would sit down to talk.

Talley also fancied himself as a stock market savant, and he traded his PA, his personal account, in rather large size. But, because of our close proximity, I knew that he usually just imitated the transactions that he saw on the trade sheets for his "smart money" clients.

On the Friday preceding the crash, Doug Talley made the trade of his life. The stock market had suffered what was then a record hundred-point decline. Talley was on the phone with one of his clients, and when he hung up, he clenched his eyes and grimaced as though he was either in pain or in ecstasy. He made a call, and then he strutted around the floor, snapping suspenders embroidered with miniature bulls, declaring an historic buying opportunity. He let it be known that, in the expectation of a big bounce-back on Monday, he had gone "all in" with his PA.

But when Talley arrived for work on Monday morning and took off his jacket, he already had half-moon-shaped sweat stains under his armpits. It was clear the stains had not been caused by the climate-controlled train ride in from Darien, Connecticut. His eyes were bloodshot, and I guessed he'd stayed up most of the night watching the Asian markets get pounded. Certainly by the time he arrived at his desk he knew that he was not going to get the bounce in his retirement account that he had dreamed of. He would remain slavishly attached to Platt's ball-and-chain for many years to come.

Most of that day, as our densely packed trading floor high above midtown Manhattan was rent with shrieks of horror, curses, and in at least one instance, hysterical laughter that sounded like sobbing, Talley sat in front of his computer screen, expressionless and silent. When the market closed, down more than five hundred points, he walked out without speaking a word.

On Tuesday, I turned up for work at my customary time: six forty-five in the morning. But while I was usually the first person on the desk, the place was thronged. I felt as though I had walked into class after an exam had already begun. It was evident that something unusual was going on when I noticed Gil Tanser, head of the institutional sales department, his face distorted by a deep frown, hovering over a small group in his glass-walled office along one side of the trading floor. He stood as the rest of the group sat, and they all seemed to be shouting into the telephone simultaneously.

Tanser was a mutton-chopped bully who had been nicknamed Genghis by his subordinates. He ran his department by fear, and he did it without ever saying much at all. Legend held that Tanser once reduced a rookie salesman to tears when, seeing the greenhorn off the phone for an extended duration, Genghis walked over and dumped the phone receiver into the colt's lap. Then he stood over the cowering salesman and waited for him to make an outgoing call, with the entire sales force as his audience.

So when Genghis roamed through the jumbled turrets of the floor, everyone scrambled to appear very, very busy. Phones would seem to rise up automatically from their cradles, and heads would snap to attention. Salesmen made furtive calls home. They even dialed one another across the desk so that they would appear to be productively engaged, making it less likely that Tanser would pick up the scent of indolence and be attracted to their vicinity. On occasion I would notice Doug Talley pick up his phone and mumble phantom gibberish quietly into thin air until Tanser clomped safely on by.

That Tuesday morning after the crash, Tom McGuire, an overgrown kid of a salesman who called on the big institutions in New York City, witnessed my arrival and saw my frozen confusion at the hubbub on the floor. He chortled and guffawed, letting out a shower of saliva that was a byproduct of his characteristic lisp. "Ha! I guess they didn't call the rookie to let him know that the world is coming to an end and to be in no later than six thirty," McGuire said before he turned back to the action.

It didn't take me long to learn that one of the firm's major clients had decided to throw in the towel and had given Platt Brothers an overnight order to liquidate a multibillion-dollar stock portfolio. Very little of the order had been sold in the overnight trade, considering the limited liquidity that generally existed for U.S. stocks in Asia and Europe in those days.

The weekend media coverage had been dismal, and the foreigners weren't buying, preferring to take the lead from Wall Street's actions. Saturday is a notoriously slow news day, and a story that might fill an inside column on the average Wednesday can get a headline on the first page of the business section on Saturday. That is exactly what happened when the market took the hundred-point dive. To add to the sour mood, the talk shows had hastily recruited economists and retired industry leaders who, being out of the game, were pleased to offer gloomy predictions that exacerbated the fear caused by Friday's steep decline and Monday's avalanche of selling.

The large sell order we'd received was supposed to be confidential, but with every Platt broker whispering and hinting into phone lines all over the world, it soon became an open secret that there would be another tidal wave of stock for sale on Tuesday when the New York market opened for trading. Legions of copycat traders, who had been forewarned, would be lined up in an attempt to sneak out their own short sales before the door slammed shut. The backdrop was set for an ugly "open," and when the New York Stock Exchange bell rang at nine thirty, stocks immediately began to drop precipitously.

Across the room, an exotic-looking fellow whose bald head gleamed a strange shade of pink under the fluorescent lights of our cramped space, stood up on the elevated platform of desks where the traders sat.

He screamed, "I am going up on two fifty Mad Dog... and I am open small." His voice was audible even over the usual bedlam that was heightened by the beginning of panic.

In my early days on the stock desk, this special language of the trade sounded like senseless babble, but slowly, through a series of questions, guesswork, and deduction, I pieced together a working knowledge of the trader's lexicon, which seemed designed to stupefy the uninformed. It wasn't all that different from the secret codes of fraternity brothers or baseball coaches who want to ensure that they are understood only by the initiated insiders.

By then, I was fluent enough to recognize that the hairless howler was trading a block of 250,000 shares of the aircraft maker, McDonnell Douglas, a company whose stock ticker was expressed by the letters MD—ergo, "Mad Dog." His reference to being "open" meant that he had bought the stock from a customer but had not yet fully placed the shares with an adequate book of offsetting buyers. That left Platt Brothers exposed as the default holder of the remaining shares. When he said "small," I also suspected that he really meant "more than I am comfortable holding."

Salesmen dutifully banged out their phone calls to offload the rump position of Mad Dog to other buyers, thereby curtailing any risk of loss to Platt and earning an "atta-boy" from their boss.

Henry Fitton, an earnest guy who only wore stiffly starched white shirts to the office and who—perhaps for that reason alone—had the reputation of being a religious type, raised his arm straight up in the air. He continued to talk excitedly into his phone and then suddenly stood and shouted toward the trading desk.

"Have a buyer of fifty Mad Dog!"

I slowly surveyed the room as this carnival of capital swirled around me. I never felt more of an outsider than when there was big action on the floor. It was as if every player snapped to attention, performing the finely choreographed role of actor or stagehand while I stood, uncertain of my lines or even how to get on stage to deliver them. I wasn't much use on an average day, but on a day like this I felt utterly worthless. Occasionally I glanced over at my would-be mentor and desk mate. I pretended not to notice, but he was in obvious distress. At last, Doug Talley leaned forward and looked me in the eyes for the first time I could remember. Embarrassed, I briefly lowered my gaze, staring at the pasty white skin covered with snaky black hair on his calf as his pants leg pulled up above the top of his sock.

"I don't know what I'm going to do," he said, talking as much to himself as to me. Then he shook his head from side to side, his lips trembled, and he turned away. I overheard his mumbled whispers as he phoned in an order to sell the shares he had purchased on Friday for his PA. When he said he was "all in," he was probably exaggerating, but it was likely that he had lost a substantial chunk of the money he had accumulated over the years from those follow-the-leader trades.

He turned back to face me. "What happened to me?" he asked—a question apparently addressed to the universe rather than to me. "How did I turn into...this?"

"Uh, are you okay?" I asked, although it was a pretty dumb question. He was definitely not okay.

"Perkins," he said, "this business is absolutely friggin' insane." He was addressing me directly, quizzically, as though I could answer him, with an intensity that made me cringe.

"Actually, I know when it started..." Talley was starting to sound like a very old man, looking back into another era. He looked terrible, and I was afraid that people were beginning to notice that he wasn't exactly his usual self.

"Uh-huh," I said encouragingly and sneaked a look. Nope, nobody else was watching what I was afraid might turn into a spectacle.

"It's all of this technology...incessantly flashing out these numbers...plusses and minuses...profits and losses...it just doesn't stop. I tell you this infection has leached out of its quarantine here and into the public at large. A *virus!*" he said. "Think about it, Perkins. Anybody—everybody—can get rich quick by simply buying the right stocks...even in a single day...*madness!*"

His strange and rambling observation completed, Talley bent over as if he were about to vomit. But he just checked that his shoelaces were firmly tied and that the bows were as even as he could make them, and then he walked out.

That was my first important lesson about financial markets. They always smell out and destroy the frailest and most vulnerable players. *The system is brutal, but it is efficient,* I thought. I wasn't feeling a lot of sympathy for Doug Talley.

By lunchtime on Tuesday, the early electricity of calamitous trading had faded into an eerie calm. The trading room suddenly became library-quiet as phone receivers stayed in their cradles and brokers stared with astonishment at their computer screens. There were minutes when it seemed as though the markets had stopped trading altogether as a dwindling phalanx of battered buyers cancelled their orders, almost in unison. I made my usual afternoon coffee run a little earlier than usual, given the predawn kickoff to the day. When I returned, McGuire was standing up across from my turret and was shouting the obvious.

"Bids are canceling. Trading has stopped," he announced, like a trumpeter blowing "Taps" and then shaking the spit out of his instrument. With his lisp, the last word sounded like "thtopped," and he was close enough that a droplet of his spittle landed on my telephone receiver.

After that, the gloom began to ebb. The Federal Reserve issued a calming statement about the U.S. economy and its willingness to lower interest rates. Before the day was over, dozens of corporations had issued press releases announcing stock buybacks to support their weakened shares. Stocks began to rise into the late afternoon. The storm had passed, a glow of sunshine was sifting through the clouds, but Doug Talley was nowhere to be seen.

Shortly after the markets closed at four o'clock, the sales and trading department of Platt Brothers filed into the elevator banks and shuffled off into the real world. Most of the traders would spend the next few hours at local watering holes. They would swap war stories from the trading day, exaggerated under the influence of alcohol. They would pass around the latest crude, off-color joke that had originated somewhere in the trading desk cosmos. They would flirt and show off, and eventually they would drag themselves home. A smaller percentage, typically the salesmen, would catch their regular trains and make it back to the suburbs in time for a sit-down meal with the family.

You could usually tell the difference between salesmen and traders because the salesmen carried briefcases and the traders had nothing but a jacket slung over their shoulder. In theory at least, sales was the brains and trading was the brawn of the operation. The idea was that the salesmen would be ferrying home research reports to study overnight so that they could engage their clients in reasoned and articulate acts of salesmanship the next morning. But having peered into the well-worn leather briefcase of my neighbor, Doug Talley, and never having seen much more than the sports pages and some breath mints, I suspected that many salesmen carried their bags just for show.

As the rookie on the sales desk, my job entailed being the last to leave the office for the day. I would pick up stray phone calls that came in after the troops had departed, typically someone's wife looking for her husband and wondering why her previous phone calls had not been returned. But usually it got quiet very quickly, and I used my solitude to review the day's activities, scrutinizing in minute detail every financial report and news item relating to my "paper portfolio," a group of stocks in a theoretical fund of my own that I followed as if I owned them.

Once, on his way out of the office, Tom McGuire had observed me lost in studious contemplation of a research report. He plopped himself down loudly in Talley's empty seat, leaned back, and burped to get my attention.

"Look here, young Nate Perkins. Do yourself a favor and don't take any of this research gibberish too seriously. If you do, you might convince yourself that we actually know something special, and that can only get you in trouble. I am going to give you some free career advice here, *so listen to me closely*," he said, stressing each word. Then he paused and squirmed in his seat as if suffering from a temporary gastric unpleasantness.

"Our job in sales is quite simple: we throw smoke in the air. All of this brainy research analysis that concludes this stock is going to go up while the other stock will go down, and that this one will outperform the other one, basically makes it hard for investors to see clearly. We promote uncertainty...and that makes investors trade more actively. Our job—in a nutshell—is to talk investors out of taking any long-term positions."

His sermon concluded, McGuire got up to leave, pushing his shirttail back into his pants as he hobbled away. Then, as if interrupted by a new thought, he turned back to face me.

"Hey, Perk. If you get a phone call from my wife, the answer is that I was with you last night, okay?" I was beginning to understand Tom McGuire in a new light—as the comic, shrewd, and deeply flawed philosopher of the business of selling stocks. I thought of Bull Wertz and what he might have thought if he had heard McGuire talking about throwing smoke in the air. It was people like Mr. Wertz who were breathing in that secondhand smoke.

When the floor was quiet enough for me to hear a stray phone ringing on the far side of the cavernous sales and trading complex and the cleaning crew swung by armed with garbage cans on wheels and feather dusters, that was my signal that it was time to go home.

As I gathered my bag and began to stroll toward the exit on that eerie and historic October evening, a phone began to buzz somewhere nearby, amongst the cluttered jumble of computer terminals and trading turrets. I paused, deliberating whether to turn back. From where I stood, I could not make out which desk's phone was ringing. It would have been easy to walk out, having given the full measure of my day's labor to Gil Tanser and the partners of Platt Brothers. I waited to see if the phone would stop ringing. It did not. Neither did I turn away. I stood motionless, waiting, listening to the steady pulsing of sound that tempted me to answer. I was a force, yet unblemished, and men of investment greatness still inhabited the hidden corners of my imagination. Stepping toward a secretarial station that sat at the end of a long row of desks, I punched the blinking yellow button on a panel of dozens of phone lines.

"Platt," I answered, in the abbreviated fashion that greeted callers to the stock desk at Platt Brothers. The voice on the other end of the line was equally curt and surprisingly high pitched.

"I am calling from Tantalus Fund for Lucas Orr," the voice said.

"Uh, sure, this is Nate Perkins," I responded instinctively. "How can I help?" Tradition on the desk held that a client in need was supported by any available salesman, though in practice I had seen that assistance was frequently extended grudgingly. The caller ignored my introduction as if he either knew me already or did not care to.

"That's right, I am calling for you. Our inquiry is exceedingly straightforward," the caller continued. "We want you to identify for us the single best investment idea that your firm's research department would recommend for clients after the market's recent decline. Take down this number and call me with an answer in the morning."

After offering up a number that commenced with a 212 area code, I heard a click and then the line was dead.

Lucas Orr! I could hardly believe that I'd almost walked away without picking up the phone. Orr ran one of the most successful and most enigmatic investment firms in the business. He was notoriously secretive: nearly every senior salesman on the desk had been assigned to call on him, and none, to my knowledge, had ever been able to get him on the phone, much less in a face-to-face meeting. Even Orr's trades were difficult to figure since he was rumored to buy a small amount of stock through one firm while selling a larger amount through another in order to cover his tracks and keep his trading positions well veiled. And this unique, famous, and mysterious investor was asking for my input on an investment proposition!

Opportunity had picked me, perhaps at random, but nevertheless I had been called. Propelled by a compulsion I could not describe, I eagerly stepped down the path that would rearrange my world. Grabbing my dingy canvas bag, which doubled as a briefcase, I headed off to the research department on the twentieth floor, taking my first tentative steps along an uncertain passageway.

∽

One of the hardest things about working on Wall Street is explaining to your family what you do for a living.

"What is it *exactly* that you are producing or manufacturing in this Wall Street job of yours?" my father had asked at a dinner one evening while winking at several of our friends and family members around the table. After the ribbing had gone on for several minutes, provoked by my father and stoked by the friendly barbs of others, I had arrived at my pat answer to this career interrogation.

"On Wall Street we manufacture ideas for the investment portfolios of America's consumers. It's no different than an apparel manufacturer merchandising his new fashions or a farmer who plants a hybrid seed to fatten the yield of his annual harvest. And we sell these ideas, just like one of Dad's auctions of surplus tractors. It's loud and it's sometimes messy. Dad, you would feel right at home."

The central construction zone for Wall Street's idea-manufacturing trade is the research department. Research transforms data into actionable trading ideas. Which industries are rising, and which are falling? Which new innovations will transform companies into booming enterprises, and which hot trends will fizzle into oblivion? Which overseas economies are the future giants, and which are fraught with political and economic risk? The answers to these questions direct trillions of dollars of capital investment flows all over the globe, and the researchers whose analysis consistently produces the right answers are worth every dollar of their rich compensation.

The sales and trading floors would be nearly vacant at six o'clock, but at this hour, the research factory at Platt Brothers would be in high gear. As I swiped my electronic access card and pushed through the glass door guarding the entrance to the intellectual core of the firm, I realized an instant too late that I had made a mistake. Straight ahead was the cavernous three-window office of Everest B. Cullman, the Director of Research. Before I could dip my shoulder and cut to the right down a corridor of exterior-facing offices, I heard a booming voice.

"Perkins! Perkins—enter my office."

Everest B. Cullman had been my entrée to Wall Street through an introduction made by my accounting professor at Columbia. Even when I didn't choose to work for him, Cullman took me under his wing, and for a while I would visit him once every couple of weeks in his office for a lunch of tuna fish sandwiches, which he would sprinkle liberally with drops of Tabasco sauce. I caught on quickly that Cullman was not disposed to short conversations, and our meetings usually stretched into the early afternoon. Once, Cullman had even invited me to join him in the partners' dining room. For a non-partner to be invited to enter the wood-paneled sanctum with its dozen tables was an honor and a chance to be showcased to the firm's top brass. I had felt every bit the outsider as I observed the strange decorum of this curious salon.

"And for you, Mr. Cullman, water with no ice and round rolls with butter, chilled. And of course there will be no tomatoes in your salad." Clearly, the black-vested waiter had memorized Cullman's dietary idiosyncrasies. But I still didn't want to work for Cullman, and I didn't want to have to explain why I was late getting back to my desk in the trading room whenever we had lunch. I had learned to make a wide berth around him during my visits to the research department.

Cullman was gazing at me like a disapproving headmaster, his eyebrows exploding in an improbable array of black and gray spikes. The outline of a smile suggested that he was glad I'd dropped by. He gestured to a chair, and I sat.

"Perkins," he declared, obviously thinking about the ramifications of the onrushing bear market, "the life of a research analyst on Wall Street today is nasty, brutish, and—above all—short." This quote rang faintly familiar to me.

He continued, "When an industry is in ascendancy, when innovation and capital formation are high, the best analysts among us represent the most valuable assets in the firm, bar none. Corporations want their strategic advice, large institutional investors seek their counsel, and small investors buy and sell stocks on their command." Cullman was practically shouting. He paused, and then he lowered his voice to a whisper.

"But when the screw turns and industries fall out of favor, when the trading commissions and M&A fees dry up, the research analyst is flung out like a soiled undergarment. This is the reality of the profession in which we toil. Make hay while the sun shines, pick your friends carefully, and save what you make," he intoned with ominous intent. Cullman was addressing me as if I was one of his research subordinates. That fact, combined with his strange delivery, made me wonder if he was mentally composed.

His sermon concluded, Cullman sat back. "Now, Perkins, why did you want to see me?" Deliberating for only a split-second, I decided not to reveal my mission.

"I actually need to get some research reports into the Fed Ex tonight," I lied. "A lot of clients are foraging for fresh money buys after this thumping." Then I jumped to my feet, and with a wave, I was off down the corridor. A picture of Cullman in soiled undergarments had gotten stuck in my mind.

Several bounds down the corridor, I ducked into a one-window office, closed the door quickly behind me, and positioned myself behind a coat rack, the only visual obstruction to the glass-walled office from the hall. In the process, I tangled myself in a wool coat that was hanging there.

An exceptionally pretty woman looked up, surprised but obviously glad to see me. She pushed her glasses up on her head, holding back her shiny, dark hair, and rubbed her eyes. Stretching her arms toward me, she knocked over a paper cup of cold coffee.

"Shit. Worst coffee in the world, and yet I buy it every day. Are you actually trying to hide there behind my coat? Is this part of the grand charade so people don't know we're seeing each other out of the office?"

"Dana," I said, "I need your help. This is a very big break."

CHAPTER TWO

The earliest Dutch settlement on the lower end of the island we now call Manhattan did not appear at first to have a promising future. Much of the land was swampy and insect-infested, and the portion of the terrain that was dry was rocky and difficult to farm. So it was not surprising that the enterprising Indians who inhabited the lands of present day Long Island and New Jersey generally steered clear of the place. But the new Dutch settlement at Fort Orange—which would later be named Albany—was growing, and fur traders up and down the Hudson were pursuing a booming trade with the Indians. When Peter Minuit was named Manhattan's first director-general, it seemed sensible to build a permanent settlement at the island's tip, which he did with the construction of Fort Amsterdam.

In setting about his building project, Minuit sought to secure a permanent ownership by formalizing a purchase of the property. But, as the island was sparsely inhabited by roaming groups of Indians, there remained some uncertainty about how to proceed. By 1626, Minuit consummated a purchase of the land for sixty Dutch guilders, conducting the transaction with a native people who, in all likelihood, had no proper claim to the land. Manhattan's reputation as a place for shady deal-making was forever sealed.

∽

Every brokerage firm on Wall Street begins its day the same way: with "the morning meeting." At precisely seven thirty in the morning, several managing partners, sitting behind a long table at a podium in the front of a large conference room, conduct a spectacle of gladiators in the Coliseum. Each research analyst has a turn at the microphone with approximately three minutes to convince the skeptical mob to buy or sell a particular stock. As soon as the analyst stops speaking, it is immediately evident whether "the call" has won the crowd over. Victory is expressed by arms raised to ask questions and pens furiously scribbling notes. Thumbs down is displayed with yawns, blank stares, and eyes turned to the sports section, tucked discreetly in the audience members' laps.

I was anxious to have the morning ritual concluded on that Wednesday, so I could return to my desk and make the most important phone call of my young career. But before the meeting began, I realized that the conference room was buzzing around me, and the reason wasn't the anticipation of the morning call. McGuire, sitting in the row in front of me, twisted his ample gut toward me with some difficulty and splattered out a few choice words.

"Did you hear about Talley?"

I grunted and shook my head. McGuire continued without waiting to find out whether I'd gotten the news. A quick glance around revealed that Talley was not in attendance.

"My wife gets a hysterical call from the soon-to-be-ex Mrs. Talley last night," McGuire said. "It turns out that our boy Talley was involved in a little hanky-panky." McGuire was sweating already, and the day had barely begun.

"Talley sent a limo to pick up his girlfriend in Connecticut last night, to bring her into the city to meet him after work for dinner and *extras*." McGuire chortled. "Dougie-boy tells the dispatcher that he is to pick up '*Mrs. Talley*,' but sends the car to his girlfriend's address instead. So the Pakistani driver gets lost, and wouldn't you know it, he gets the dispatcher to call the Talley residence to ask for directions." Ears perked up around us at this fascinating twist in McGuire's tale.

"Ha, can you imagine Mrs. Talley's surprise when she discovers that her husband has sent a car to pick *her* up, but it just happens that the car is going to an address with which she is unfamiliar?"

The morning meeting was gaveled to order, but McGuire had no intention of interrupting himself, and he had now garnered the attention of two full rows. Even the finely starched Henry Fitton was paying rapt attention to the unfolding saga.

"Well, the genuine Mrs. Talley jumps in her car, races to the address she gets from the dispatcher, and arrives just as our friend Ahmed pulls in to pick up Talley's girlfriend. The two 'Mrs. Talleys' then proceed to scream at each other as Ahmed sits there, stunned. They're both so mad that Talley's girlfriend sends Ahmed away, and Mrs. Talley goes home and starts putting together a list of killer divorce lawyers. Meanwhile, Talley is sitting at the Pierre with a bottle of Dom Perignon in a bucket of ice and no clue as to what is going on in Darien!" As laughter erupted in the middle rows of the conference room, Everest Cullman rose from his chair at the center of the podium and shouted.

"Quiet!"

The research call offered relatively meager sustenance that morning. One of the senior traders commented on the whipsaw trading activity in convoluted terms that didn't offer any confident predictions about the prospects for the day ahead. The senior economist droned on nasally about how the stock market crash would likely affect consumer spending and GDP forecasts, seemingly aiming his remarks at a young blonde associate sitting cross-legged in the front row. Interest picked up moderately when a biotechnology analyst downgraded his opinion of every stock on his coverage list after having read an over-the-top bullish report on the industry in the critically influential forum of an in-flight airline magazine.

The final speaker was a dark-haired beauty. She was unfamiliar to most of the brokers in the room, and Cullman took the lead by introducing her.

"I can appreciate that chemicals might not be the favorite topic *du jour* amongst the sales force," he said in his plodding and deliberate delivery. "But I ask for your indulgence on the presentation that will follow. Ms. Dana Rocca is a proud new addition to the research staff, and she has come up with some worthwhile insights on her industry."

The room perked up instantly; a new face was always interesting. And a pretty face and a good figure certainly did not hurt when it came to attracting attention from the mostly male audience. No one seemed to be taking notes, and they might not have been listening, but that didn't mean they weren't looking.

I was anxious to get back to my telephone, and I was the first to exit the room when the meeting adjourned. I wasn't sure when, or if, Talley would be coming into the office after the debacles of the previous day and night, but I was eager to make my phone call to Lucas Orr before Talley had settled into the seat adjacent to mine. I knew that I was violating a cardinal rule of the business: you don't call on another broker's client without his approval. But since I didn't know for whom that amber light had been flashing, I decided that it was meant for me. Caring little about tradition or treachery, I took a deep breath and dialed.

When the phone rang in the executive offices of an office tower on Park Avenue, a sturdy male voice answered on the first ring.

"Tantalus Fund."

I momentarily forgot the short speech that I had rehearsed dozens of times over the last eight hours. It was as if someone had dropped a blanket over my brain.

"Uh, this is Nate Perkins from Platt Brothers," I blurted out. "Lucas Orr is expecting my call. I spoke to one of his people last night."

"Hold please," the receptionist answered.

29

I sat with the receiver pressed hard against my ear. I felt as though everyone in the room was watching me. The blood was ebbing from my head as the large digital clock over the trading desk ticked away seconds articulated in flashing pulses of neon green.

"Well, what have you got?" I heard the high-pitched voice I recognized from the night before. Then the blanket lifted, and my mind was suddenly as clear as it had ever been. I went straight to the point.

"I have something very, very interesting for you to consider," I said, pausing twice to stress the word "very." I continued, "This is an undiscovered situation, a company that has just been spun off by a larger corporation, so the business is not well understood in the market, and the shares are way too cheap. This company also has some very positive business developments that lie just ahead."

"We can do our own research. What is the company?" the squeaky voice on the line demanded.

"Well, here is the thing," I said, matching his excitability with a steady calm. "I can't do this over the phone. I am going to have to present this idea directly to Mr. Orr, and I am going to have to do it at your office." I moved the receiver away from my mouth so that Squeaky could not hear me gasping for fresh oxygen.

"What!" My phone was filled with several minutes of colorful expletives. I said nothing, shocked by the insolence of my plan. When it became clear that we were at a standstill, Orr's man put the phone on hold and went to seek a higher authority. It seemed like minutes elapsed as I waited on a phone line where no music played. I thought maybe Orr's lieutenant had hung up in response to my audacity.

"Okay, Luc will see you for ten minutes. Be here at four o'clock."

༄

Tantalus Fund occupied the entire top floor of a black office tower a ten-minute walk from my office. The façade of the magnificent structure had the effect of mirrored sunglasses, and I felt as though the eyes within were staring down on me while I could not see them. Access to the firm involved two important security checks. First, I navigated a lobby guard who escorted me to a private elevator that only stopped on the forty-ninth floor. Upon arriving at the building's summit, I stepped into an empty hallway. A heavy wooden door with bronze hinges, made to look as though it came out of an Italian palazzo, stood at the end of the hallway, and a ceiling camera tracked my every move as I paced, waiting for something to happen. Shortly, a bolt clicked, and I entered a small, wood-paneled reception area.

A thick-necked man, who looked like the 1930s movie prototype of a New York City Irish cop, was standing to greet me. Wordlessly, he pointed to a dark green sofa, and I sat down and surveyed my surroundings. My heart was pounding as I contemplated my unthinkable circumstances. Momentarily, I was falling back in time, recognizing a strange out-of-body sensation that often accompanied my moments of exaltation.

Floating nearby, I felt as if I was watching Nate Perkins sitting on the sofa, staring at a massive canvas that filled most of the adjacent wall. It was painted in ominous dark tones, and it depicted a bearded old man on his knees, a look of despair cast across his wrinkled brow. One hand reached up, trying to grasp plump apples dangling from the tree limbs just out of his reach. With equal desperation, his other hand reached down, trying to cup water from a stream on the ground. That too lay just barely out of his reach. Wresting my gaze from the hypnotic spell of the portrait of misery and frustration, I quickly came under the steely glare of a series of carved African masks that adorned the wall to my other side. The angry charcoal eyes seemed to survey both Nates interchangeably—the Nate on the sofa and the other Nate who floated outside his body—as though the spirits in the masks were deliberating our fate.

"Come," the reception area attendant said, and he beckoned me toward another door. I suspected his role was more to provide security than to greet guests or take messages. I followed him down a long hallway with museum-quality lighting illuminating magnificent artwork and a silence that, in itself, seemed opulent.

Lucas Orr occupied a cavernous office with massive slanted window panels covering two entire walls. The views over the Manhattan landscape must have been spectacular, but the blinds had all been drawn, lending an air of containment. There were no ceiling lights in the large space, which was illuminated entirely from the radiance emitted by four dimly-lit corner table lamps and one bronze banker's lamp with a frosted shade of emerald green that sat on Orr's desk. The room's expansiveness and limited lighting made for a hospitable home to shadows. I was greeted by a delicately-built, rumpled young man, and from his voice I recognized my squeaky caller from the previous night. He introduced himself as Ted Newman and then retreated to a high-backed leather sofa, which sat facing Orr but was some twenty feet away from the boss.

Orr's desk was clean, with only the lamp, a telephone, and a computer monitor. He stood to one side of the desk, gesturing for me to come forward. As I stood in front of him, we studied each other without speaking. He was not what I expected. Standing before me was a trim man of medium height who had not removed his suit jacket. On Wall Street, this was most unusual. The popular image of men in suits, which I had carried with me from Kansas, was entirely wrong. From the CEO on down, every man at Platt Brothers took off his jacket when he arrived in the morning and spent the day strutting around in expensive, custom-made shirts that never seemed to lose their starch. Top buttons remained buttoned and silk ties from Hermès or shops on Saville Row in London stayed neatly tied, but nobody in the know wore a jacket unless he was meeting with a client.

Orr's hair was blond, verging on brown, and perfectly cut. Catching a quick glimpse of his head from the side, I noticed he also had a cowlick. When the light of his desk lamp reflected true against his face, I could tell that his skin was quite pale, but as he stepped slightly to one side, out of the direct light, his complexion suddenly darkened. His frame was narrow, but his face was distinguished by a strong, chiseled jaw that resonated strength, and he moved with the confidence of an athlete. They say you can see into a man's soul by studying his face. But as I looked into his clear gray-blue eyes, which bulged a trifle too prominently, it occurred to me how little a man's face actually gives away. I could have been looking into the eyes of a genius or a thief.

"Your impressive portrait of Tantalus in the waiting room is technically inaccurate," I offered as my opening salvo. A nearly imperceptible twitch of Orr's eyebrow suggested I should continue.

"Tantalus was once most favored by his father, Zeus, and admitted to the banquets of the gods. But later he was cast out to Hades, damned to a unique and eternal punishment: he was forced to stand chin-deep in water with fruits just above his head. When he reached down to drink, the water receded and when he reached up to eat, the fruit branches were lifted out of his reach. But your rendering has Tantalus reaching for both food and water simultaneously. He should be reaching for one or the other," I concluded, quite pleased with my recital. It seemed like a good omen that Lucas Orr and I might share a fascination with Greek mythology. Orr watched me without blinking.

"Impressive knowledge of the Greek gods," he said at last as he sat down. "Perhaps you should consider that this Tantalus is more ambitious. And do you know why he was banished to Hades?"

Since I did not know the answer, I deflected the conversation. "Shall we talk about Simpson Chemical?"

I had forgotten Ted Newman's presence when he piped up from across the room, "Good. We don't have much time, so let's get on with it." My performance began with a straightforward narrative as I remained standing.

"Simpson Chemical is owned by Textor, the Houston oil company. Textor, having spent the last ten years buying up a hodgepodge of businesses in order to diversify, has recently brought in a new management team that has now decided to clean house and get back to its primary business of oil and gas. So they are divesting all non-core operations. Simpson's management team used this opportunity to buy the company from the parent in a leveraged buyout, funded with about a billion dollars of borrowed money. The lenders who provided the debt financing were given warrants to buy 20 percent of the stock in the company as an added inducement. Here's where it gets interesting." I paused briefly for emphasis.

"The institutions that now own these warrants are largely a group of insurance companies and banks with little knowledge or interest in the equity play, and they have started selling the warrants into the marketplace. And since there are no public shares trading today, no research coverage, and little understanding of Simpson's operations, the warrants are trading at a fraction of what they are worth."

Orr sat expressionless, but I was standing half-turned, so my back wasn't to Newman, and I noticed he was leaning forward on the sofa. My tutorial continued.

"Simpson's main product is surfactants, chemical elements that are used in the detergent industry. Demand for these products is booming, particularly due to growing consumer demand in the emerging markets. The global capacity of these chemicals is woefully short and likely to stay that way since building these plants is no small undertaking. I have strong reason to believe that Simpson will dramatically increase their prices in the next few weeks, and the cash flow of this business will explode upward in the coming year." Orr remained seemingly unmoved.

"Let's talk numbers," I continued. "There are twenty million Simpson warrants, and they are trading today at around three dollars each. We...uh...I believe that this company will probably do an initial public offering of shares within the next six months, on the back of very strong financial reports, with a valuation for the company approaching one point five billion dollars."

Orr ran the math instantaneously. "The warrant valuation says the company is worth three hundred million dollars, and you are telling me that it is actually worth closer to five times that amount! So the warrants currently trading for three dollars will be worth fifteen dollars in relatively short order?"

"That is exactly what I am saying," I responded with the supreme confidence of an insider.

"And how, precisely, do you have this level of insight since neither the esteemed Platt Brothers nor any other Wall Street

firm provides research coverage on the company?" Orr shot
back.

"You asked me for a great investment idea, not for a
bibliography of my sources," I volleyed back with a forcefulness
that I hoped would impress. Orr grinned—it was the first time
he had shown more than the slightest hint of warmth—and
I knew the interview was over. I was hustled from the office
down the same silent hallway, and again I did not see anyone. It
struck me that the employees of Tantalus were concealed, just
like the view out of Lucas Orr's reflecting window.

CHAPTER THREE

Almost two hundred years after Henry Hudson's arrival in New York Harbor, a young boy, who was descended from an indentured servant of Dutch ancestry, dropped out of school on Staten Island to work for his father. The father and son labored together in the rough-and-tumble ferry trade that populated the waterways around the thriving city that had been renamed New York when the Dutch settlement fell under British control. By the age of sixteen, the boy was physically strong, mentally hardened, and industrious. Driven by an innate brashness that bordered on arrogance, he decided to strike out on his own. The young entrepreneur purchased a small boat with his meager savings and struck out to make his name. Braving the foulest weather conditions at any hour, he labored tirelessly in search of paying freight. He soon developed a reputation for reliable service at the best prices, an operating philosophy that would serve him well as his enterprise grew to a monumental size.

The boy's name was Cornelius Vanderbilt; later he would be known as "the Commodore," although his early exploits as a merchant captain would prove to be a small footnote in the large life that was to follow.

∽

It was nearly one o'clock in the morning when I ascended two flights of stairs and let myself into a darkened, railroad-style apartment in New Jersey, located just down the street from Frank Sinatra's childhood home. It had been an unusual late night of drinking with the traders, an evening prolonged by the giddy aura that I felt, as if I had joined a special club after my meeting with Lucas Orr that afternoon. At some point well into the revelry, I remembered I had promised Dana I would make the trek to her apartment across the river in Hoboken to report on my meeting. The thirty-minute bus ride would entail a dreaded trek through the dingy and vagrant-filled Port Authority Bus Terminal, but the destination would justify the journey.

Dana Rocca and I had both entered the ranks of Platt Brothers over the summer, along with another dozen or so MBAs. When they put our group through a two-week off-site training assessment, Dana had been our group's standout. With her quick wit and a sophisticated charm that seemed to come naturally, she had the tools to succeed in a man's world. I liked her instantly and was surprised when she responded to my tentative flirtations. When our relationship had moved beyond mere friendship, we had agreed that it was a good idea to keep our connection out of the public eye since no good could come from its disclosure within the walls of our employer. I wondered on several occasions whether there might actually be a policy that prohibited dating someone in the firm, but I certainly wasn't going to ask. After our brief training orientation was over, we were each placed in the department where we had hoped to work. I went to Institutional Equities, and Dana went to Equity Research.

I retrieved the key from a small ledge above the doorway and shuffled forward in the dark, stripping off my clothes before climbing into the double bed where Dana was sleeping soundly. As I pulled the sheets over us, my hands reached out to touch her cheek, trying to wake her gently. I whispered into her ear as I pressed my body against the flesh that had tantalized so many roving eyes at the Platt Brothers morning meeting.

"Thank you," I said.

She stretched her neck, moaned softly, and then turned over to face me. There was enough light in the room, so I could see that her eyes were open, if just barely.

"You entered the sanctum of the Man of Mystery and emerged to live another day?" She spoke with a sleepy croak in her voice, and she cleared her throat. "You didn't tell him where you got the idea, did you?" she asked.

"I told him that my sources belonged to me...only me," I said, pulling her closer. In a tone that mimicked the company rulebook, I continued, "I know that you haven't officially published on the company yet, and the research department policy is that all ideas have to be vetted internally before reports can be issued for client consumption."

"And what about my inaugural presentation to the sales force this morning on the chemical industry?" she asked, sounding more alert.

"Honey, as far as I am concerned, you might well have been speaking Urdu."

She giggled, and then we both surrendered to the pleasures of a warm bed on a cold night.

∽

The months that followed the crash were cold and dismal in the office, which made me appreciate Dana's energetic companionship. In her presence I was interchangeable as a dance partner for salsa lessons or as a sidekick on a weekend romp for apple picking. Sometimes we went together to one of the expensive charity dinners to which Platt Brothers had bought a couple of tables. Typically the seats were filled with younger staffers who found the clothes, the jewels, and the big names exciting, while the more seasoned managing directors had been to so many of those dinners they were ready to give away their dinner jackets.

Though stock prices did recover somewhat in the uncertain post-crash period, business activity was down substantially. All the salesmen clung anxiously to their client relationships like marooned sailors clutching a last hunk of hardtack. No one knew what lay ahead. In the absence of my own significant Rolodex of clients, I began to call Ted Newman at Tantalus every few days, and I was surprised when he responded to my phone calls with some interest. One day, about two weeks into my courtship, Tantalus Fund appeared on my daily commission run, indicating that I had become the official salesman to the account. No one ever spoke to me about the change, and I never bothered to find out who had been the previous salesman of record.

It soon became clear to me that I needed to read Platt's research reports extremely diligently before reporting on them as Newman would typically ask me to critique the quality of the analysis. I had the impression that he was taking notes every time we spoke. Sometimes he would also ask for my opinions about the quality of Platt's research analysts. Once, when he asked me what I thought about the work of Dana Rocca, I blustered before stumbling through a noncommittal response. He paused as if to pursue a follow-up question, but then he decided against it.

My conversations with Newman excited my interest in the blunt power of knowledge. I caught small glimpses of the daunting and brilliant investment operation that Lucas Orr managed. Newman would occasionally hint at ideas they were considering and projects they were undertaking, luring me inside the mysterious den of Tantalus until I felt like a covetous voyeur. I wanted more.

One Friday afternoon, when the markets were slow and most of the players were preparing to head out for a three-day weekend, Newman called me to chat. He seemed unusually jocular and unhurried, and we bantered aimlessly before I decided to try out one of the jokes I had picked up from my casual eavesdropping on the sales pitch of a more seasoned peddler. I had come to understand that on Wall Street, jokes were not only as ubiquitous as fruit flies, but they were also as essential as liquor at a cocktail party. When the client conversation was a little threadbare, a joke could serve as the crucial social lubricant to extend the vital relationship-building exposure to a paying customer.

"So, Ted, I guess you realize that business has gotten a little tough on Wall Street?" I began. Newman grunted, not really sure where I was going with the conversation.

"Do you know what you call a hotshot stockbroker in suspenders these days?" I paused for effect, attempting to emulate the delivery I had heard a senior broker deliver earlier in the day.

"Waiter." I accentuated the punch line with a laugh of my own—as if that would make the gag funnier.

Newman snorted, which could be construed as a feeble attempt to chuckle, and then he paused. I wasn't sure whether he didn't get the joke or thought my attempt at self-deprecation was lame. Perhaps my presentation was not adroit enough. Almost casually, he steered the conversation to my opinions on the hotel industry.

"It looks like Bonham Corporation is probably going to be taken over," Newman offered nonchalantly. "We always thought their properties were worth far more than the stock price."

The statement was delivered so matter-of-factly I couldn't tell if he was revealing a valued insight or a conventional and widespread opinion. The following week, I decided he was doing me a favor, and concluding that a sufficient amount of time had elapsed, I played the hunch. I committed the whole of my paltry life savings to purchasing five hundred shares of Bonham common stock.

Ten days later, the lead financial story reported that Bonham Corporation had agreed to an acquisition by a large European hotel operator for a 50 percent price premium. My ego swelled when I heard the news. Striding across the noisy trading floor, I felt like I belonged. I was becoming a player in the lucrative and guilt-tinged money game.

In the late fall, in response to the crash, which had done considerable damage all over the Street, Platt Brothers initiated a RIF, a reduction-in-force, that eliminated Doug Talley's job. There was no more terrifying sight on the trading floor than the appearance of Pierre from the human resources department, a lanky, dark-haired man of no more than forty who walked with a stoop and always carried a thick, black notebook tucked under his arm. He arrived like the grim reaper, on a day when the market was up sixty points, to walk Talley to a conference room for a brief exit interview and to describe his severance arrangement. HR served as an innocuous cost center most of the time, tucked somewhere into the bowels of the firm in cluttered space with obstructed window views. But when job cutbacks were called for, Pierre and his team of paper shufflers surged to life, briefly bestowed with the fearsome power of the sword.

I'm not sure whether the top brass at Platt Brothers thought people felt better about being "riffed" than they did about being "fired," but it didn't look that way when the people who had been asked to leave were escorted from the building. By firing people before bonuses were announced in December, the firm stiffed the terminated employees out of a year's worth of compensation, paying severance in lieu of bonus. I thought about the fact that Talley had scored a Wall Street hat-trick by losing a large chunk of his investment portfolio, his wife, who had sued him for divorce after the limousine episode, and his job in such a short span. I learned another important Wall Street lesson: misfortune travels in bunches.

When people found out that Lucky Garcia had also been terminated, I heard a few salesmen say that this was a very bad omen. Lucky was an unimportant player in the firm who had obtained his nickname because of typical Wall Street superstition. Lucky, whose real name was José, was an earnest kid from the Bronx whose mother had worked for many years as a custodian, cleaning the reams of paper and pizza boxes and other refuse that littered the trading floor after any ordinary business day at Platt Brothers. A few years back, Lucky's mom had convinced one of the senior traders to interview her son for a support job in operations, where he would be responsible for picking up trading tickets from the trading desk and key-punching them into a computer terminal to ensure the trade was properly recorded on the firm's books.

The day that José Garcia had come in for his interview had been one of the most raucous and profitable trading days in the firm's history. José sat in a seat next to the trading desk for six hours without moving, his wide department store tie clearly out of place in a world of thin slivers of silk and starched shirts. Amidst the frenzy, José and his interview had been simply overlooked. But when four o'clock arrived and the bloated P&L had been totaled and celebrated, someone finally noticed that he was still sitting there patiently. In the giddy celebratory atmosphere of that trading day, they had hired José on the spot without so much as a conversation and promptly nicknamed him "Lucky." But Pierre from HR didn't think much about luck when he needed to make his numbers.

Having successfully diminished some of the extra weight that might otherwise have exacted a claim on the profit pool, HR receded back to its grotto, allowing Platt's bonus ritual to proceed. In our division, Gil Tanser sat in his office with a stack of papers while salesmen filed in and out for most of the day. You could usually tell the level of an employee's disappointment by the duration of the meeting. Long meeting—bad news. Short meeting—good news. Late in the afternoon, when it was my turn to receive "the number," my expectations were not high, given my short tenure and the fragile state of the markets. I was apprehensive when I sat down for my meeting with Tanser.

"Lucas Orr apparently likes the work you have been doing covering their account, Perkins," Tanser said bluntly and without any hint of compliment. He sounded resentful of my early success. "They have upped their trading volumes with us substantially; don't screw it up."

"Thank you," I said instinctively when Tanser announced my number, handing me a sheet of paper that confirmed the bonus. I realized immediately that expressing gratitude was a mistake because I had observed that most of the big hitters carried a permanent swagger of entitlement. Immediately I retreated to the trading floor bathroom, where a boxer's punching bag hung in a corner. Locking myself in the center stall, I sat down and stared at the plain white sheet of paper that described the terms of my fifty-thousand-dollar bonus.

I was bewitched by the power of the numbers printed in black and white, and all mine.

I had been unable to conceal a foolish grin as I returned to my desk, and McGuire blurted out, "Hey, look, Perk is smiling. They must have bumped him up to five digits!" And then he performed an orchestrated belly laugh for the entire room.

"Don't look back; I am gaining on you," I shot back to McGuire in response.

Later in the week, McGuire pulled me into a small conference room and furtively revealed to me the bonus numbers for a good part of the sales department. The day of paying employees by check was long over; we just got a pay stub indicating that a direct deposit had been made into our bank accounts. To satisfy his personal curiosity about what everyone else got paid, McGuire had developed the nasty habit of filching the first pay stub that arrived in the inbox of his unsuspecting colleagues following bonus day. He had somehow decided that I was to be his confidante, a colleague to whom he could reveal his innermost thoughts and vices.

"You know, Perk," he said, "I don't really have that MBA degree from Darden."

As I studied McGuire, his corpulence began to strike me as less benevolent, less genial.

"It isn't just that I didn't graduate. I never even attended the school. But that's okay because they will never check it out."

"What! Really?" I stared in disbelief.

"A lesson for you here, Perk. If you are going to tell a lie in this business, make sure that it's a doozy, so whopping that no one could imagine that you had the balls to simply make it up. Otherwise, don't even bother."

I had also become aware through McGuire's penchant for repeating gossip that other members of the sales force had grown to resent me because I had been assigned coverage of Tantalus. The biggest accounts were ordinarily the province of the most senior salesmen. Rookies like me were supposed to back up their betters on these large accounts and develop relatively few small-fry accounts of their own to call on. Nevertheless, I plowed forward, knowing that as long as I stayed in the good graces of Lucas Orr, I was inoculated against pettiness and ill-feeling inside my firm.

As the New York winter melted into spring and the tables were hauled out onto sidewalk cafes, I began to yearn for another encounter with the curious and enticing Lucas Orr. And then one Friday afternoon, when most of the Platt Brothers stock department had already left for the weekend, the amber ring light on my phone lit up as if on cue, and somehow I knew who was calling. The burly male voice on the phone said, "Hold for Luc Orr."

When we were connected, even before Orr could utter a word of introduction, I blurted out, "I know why Tantalus was banished to eternal suffering."

"I am listening," responded the faintly familiar voice on the other end of the line.

"Tantalus was banished because he betrayed the trust of Zeus and shared the secrets of the gods with mere mortals."

I was proud that I had eliminated the need for awkward introductory small talk by taking the initiative.

"I want you to come over to my office," Orr said, redirecting the conversation. I inhaled.

"When?" I asked.

"Now," he said.

After my regular conversations with Ted Newman, I had the feeling that this rendezvous would be altogether different than my first meeting. Despite the uneasy feeling that Lucas Orr and Tantalus were more than I could handle, I said blithely, "On my way."

The last time I was in Orr's office, I had stood throughout the interview. This time, he invited me to sit in a chair facing him. And unlike our first meeting, we were alone. The room struck me as even darker than I recollected from our first meeting. Glancing down at my feet, I noticed tired leather peeking through the scrapes of my stale brown shoes. I tucked my feet behind me, hoping Orr wouldn't notice how badly I needed a shoeshine.

"I will be direct," said Orr. "I am prepared to offer you a position to work with us here at Tantalus. We will double your present compensation to one hundred fifty thousand dollars, and you will be in a position to make multiples of that amount over time, depending on the quality of your work." It struck me as odd that Orr knew the precise details of my most recent earnings, but by then I had the sense that he could find out pretty much anything he wanted to know and that his system was considerably more sophisticated than rummaging around for pay stubs.

"You will report directly to me in a role similar to that you have observed Newman perform. This job will fascinate you. This job will stimulate you. This job will change your life."

Orr delivered his offer with an air of such divine authority that I was too stunned to ask how the job would change my life. I looked at him closely, appraising him now for the second time. As I studied Orr, he suddenly leaned back in his chair away from the illumination of his green-shaded desk lamp, casting a long shadow across his face. His slender frame appeared more athletic than I remembered from our first meeting, though the movement of his upper body was constricted by his well-tailored dark suit jacket as it had been during our first meeting. His fair hair flowed back from his brow in waves that seemed neither random nor arranged. As Orr leaned forward again, into the radiance bathing his desk, I could see that his teeth were neat and white but were slightly small for his mouth.

"Why me?" I asked to buy myself some seconds to think.

Orr didn't hesitate. "One: you have good instincts, as evidenced by the Simpson Chemical idea. The warrants we bought at an average price of four dollars are now trading at eighteen dollars. Two: you work hard. Do you think it's by coincidence that we first called you one night when I knew that the only person likely left on the desk was either the lowest man in the pecking order or the most ambitious? I discovered both were true. And three: you are bold, as evidenced by the brash way you invited yourself over to deliver an answer in person. I will need that quality."

On Monday morning, I walked into Gil Tanser's office before he had finished his first cup of coffee, and I resigned. He seemed stunned, and as I looked down on his broad, bald scalp and watched several rows of wrinkles form, I knew there was nothing he could do or say. I was now a customer of his firm, and a very important one at that. As he stumbled uncomfortably through a short farewell speech, my mind drifted to the time when, as an eight-year-old, I had decided to climb the ladder to the top of a diving platform on a guest visit to a fancy swim club. As I stood thirty feet above the water, looking down, a small crowd gathered below and chanted, "Jump." Dazed by the gathering spectators and too embarrassed to climb back down, I jumped.

After I walked out of Tanser's office, I logged a quick call to Dana. I had told her about my decision the night before, and we had celebrated over the most expensive dinner tab I had ever paid. Not knowing anything about wine, I had ordered a bottle of Brunello with a hundred-dollar price tag and repeatedly toasted Dana's brilliance.

When she answered the phone, I said, "The deed is done. I am taking the plunge—preparing to plumb the dark spaces of the unknown."

"Good luck, Nate," she said. "Don't forget to bring your flashlight—or a torch."

After that, I shook a few hands around the floor and walked right out of Platt Brothers. My eight-month career as a stockbroker was over, and I was about to enter a strange new realm.

I did not run into Orr during my first two weeks working at Tantalus, even though I'd been given an office next to Ted Newman's, which was two down from Orr's. On several occasions I glanced into Orr's office, but I never saw him. I spent most of my days hanging around Newman, trying to gain a quick understanding of the role they expected me to play in the opaque enterprise I had joined.

Newman operated like a central clearinghouse for information within Tantalus. He expertly extracted knowledge from a network of sources that touched every nook of the financial markets and the real economy. He would routinely conduct twenty or more phone conversations in a day, plucking short snippets of information as if he were extracting the meat from a lobster's claws. Newman would converse with brokers on Wall Street in his Chihuahua bark as he ferreted out information. He would speak to research analysts, probing for salient and new developments in their industries. When he spoke to executives who ran large companies, he knew how to dance delicately around topics, to decipher trends without tripping his unwitting informants into the charged wire that involved the conscious disclosure of insider information. After these conversations, he would turn to me, briefly describe his interview tactics, and recap the significance of what he learned from each source.

I was amazed when I realized that very little that transpired in Newman's conversations was ever committed to text. He carried a hard-backed red notebook in which he scribbled concise summary notes, always omitting names and dates. There was never any computer record of these investment discussions, and use of the Tantalus internal network was expressly prohibited for the exchange of investment-related information with parties inside or outside the firm.

On my first day serving my new master, in addition to submitting to a urine test and providing fingerprints, I had been asked to sign a code of conduct. I signed a particularly stiff confidentiality agreement that I would never disclose internal matters to any outsider or take any firm property outside of the office. I had been issued my own hard-backed red notebook, which was subject to random inspection by an inscrutable, fuzzy-haired senior legal officer of the firm, Ashton Malpas, who occupied the office just outside Orr's door. Despite our oath of allegiance to Tantalus, I was surprised how little information I was given about the nature of the firm's operation. The firm had no marketing department, having apparently ceased accepting new clients long before I arrived. The size of the investment pool was also uncertain, at least to me. I did not gain much additional insight when I asked Newman.

"The number is over a billion—I think. And it's mostly now Orr's money from retained earnings, along with a small group of handpicked clients who don't ask any questions. He gave most of the early investors their money back when he stopped needing outside capital to feed the machine."

Newman explained his job and mine in very simple terms. We served as filters of information to the master. Our job was to nourish, build, and ultimately exploit the firm's extensive network of sources, funneling vast amounts of information. We were expected to separate the irrelevant from the instructive and present our most promising nuggets to Orr for his deliberation and, ultimately, for action.

Newman remained restrained and "all business" during the long hours we spent together. After several months on the job, I was occasionally able to convince him to join me for a quick lunch outside the office. As we strolled in the broad, sun-splashed expanse of Park Avenue, his demeanor would sometimes thaw, and our conversation would become more ordinary. I was able to learn that he had been preordained to work in finance; his father and grandfather had both toiled for long careers as stockbrokers. Upon graduating from Yale and Harvard Business School several years back, he was one of the few students who had been successful in obtaining the rare job on the lucrative "buy side" of Wall Street at the investment firms who bought securities for their client portfolios. Most of his classmates who went to work on Wall Street had to settle for the more pedestrian and readily available jobs on the "sell side," like the one I'd held at Platt. His parents had been very proud of Ted when he joined Lucas Orr's enterprise.

I used our private moments together to probe Newman for information about Orr. Who was he? Where did he come from? What motivated him? What made him so good at what he did? My colleague typically deflected these advances.

"Luc doesn't like to see a lot of fraternization between his employees," he mentioned to me during one lunch as we sat at a table on the edge of the neatly manicured lawns of Bryant Park, behind the New York Public Library. "I've pieced together that he grew up somewhere 'out there'—I don't even know what state. He was raised without a father, and his mother worked menial jobs—sounds like his childhood was a little bleak, but ordinary enough that there isn't much to talk about."

"How did he get his start in the business?" I inquired, using the affable moment to press for more.

"Here's what I know. He graduated from City College with a degree in accounting and got a job working for a small investment operation named Colesmith Capital. Leonard Colesmith was too well-bred to play the part of bloodthirsty financial buccaneer. He did recognize Orr's gift, though, and brought him over to help manage the investments. Within two years, Colesmith had retired and Orr had taken over the business."

"Two years? Quick work, I guess. So when did Luc emerge to investment greatness?" I asked. The question made me sound like an awestruck teenage fan, but I was keen for Newman to keep talking.

"Every great investor can probably identify the single investment that launched him from side-street anonymity into main-street prominence. For Orr it would have to be Broadway Video." Newman paused, and I hoped he would continue.

"Broadway Video rode the boom in the movie rental industry that followed the mass adoption of the VCR. The company grew helter-skelter, from one store to several thousand within a very short number of years, financing the growth almost entirely with debt. They overexpanded, hit the wall almost as quickly, and the company went bankrupt. Orr moved in and scooped up the bank debt and creditor claims and ended up owning the company after the ensuing restructuring. Everyone thought he was nuts at the time, but he cut costs, closed the marginal stores, and spruced up the rest. It didn't take long before he had the business spewing cash again. But the real gem in the business was the database of over a million customers. Orr spent a boatload of money mining the customer data for targeted marketing opportunities and special promotions. These efforts succeeded beyond his dreams." Newman smiled wryly and added, "And of course there is the power that comes from knowing what kind of movies people consume in their private hours."

"But we don't do restructuring or mergers and acquisitions here," I said.

"That was then; this is now," Newman answered abruptly. "Success can sometimes lead you in new directions." A breeze rustled through the trees shading our table, and Newman hastily bundled the remnants of a ham and cheese sandwich into his brown paper bag.

"It's time to return to the mother ship," he said, without any hint of joy. "Luc wants to meet with us this afternoon."

We walked in silence the handful of blocks back to our offices on Park Avenue. As we mounted the steps that led to the elevated plaza entrance to the building, Newman turned to me and softly spoke a single word. "Penumbra."

The quizzical look on my face revealed that this was not one of the SAT vocabulary words still lodged in the unused recesses of my cerebral cortex, so my tutor followed up with a definition.

"Penumbra, translated literally from the Latin, means 'almost-shadow.' It represents the imperfect shaded spot that lies outside the well-defined shadow cast by an opaque body, like a planet. It is a place of partial light and partial darkness."

I gaped, knowing that Newman was opening up to me in a way that I suspected he had not intended.

"Penumbra, Nate, is where the business life of New York happens. And it is decidedly where Lucas Orr lives and thrives."

༄

"I think your initial training is complete," Orr told me when Newman and I had gathered in his office that afternoon. He had slightly raised the blinds shading one of his windows, and a beam of light illuminated a patch of the dark, wide plank floor without touching any of the three of us. Orr continued.

"Working alongside Newman has sharpened your understanding of our practice. You are more aware of how we forage and how we hunt. Of course, you still have much to learn. In the next phase of your development, I will be asking you to take the lead on a handful of projects, Nate."

It was the first time Lucas Orr had ever addressed me by my first name. I said nothing, knowing that Orr's charge was not yet concluded.

"First, I will need you to understand something about our investment operation. Our approach to investing is...different." Orr paused to study me.

"The purchase of the Simpson Chemical warrants would represent an exception to our usual practice. How familiar are you with short selling?" Orr bared two neat rows of lucent teeth and clicked them together a couple of times as he stared at me intently, awaiting a response.

"Well...uh...I of course am familiar with short selling," I responded and recited my lesson. "Short selling is the practice of selling shares that you do not own in an attempt to profit, on the belief that they will fall in price," I said. "I guess you can say that short selling is essentially the opposite of buying a stock in the belief it will appreciate in value."

Orr was unmoved, suggesting to me that I should continue speaking. "A short seller contracts with a brokerage firm to borrow shares that the firm holds in their inventory and then sells those shares into the market at the prevailing price. If the shares subsequently decline in value, the short seller can lock in the decline as a profit by purchasing the shares at the lower price and returning them to the brokerage firm from which he contracted the original borrow. But if the price goes up after a short sale, every dollar of appreciation represents a dollar of loss to the short seller."

I suddenly remembered, and mechanically repeated, a brief ditty that a Columbia B-school professor had used in his tutorial of the craft: "He who sells what isn't his own buys it back or goes to prison."

"You have provided an accurate textbook explanation," Orr retorted. "But how familiar are you with the strategies for identifying these sorts of opportunities? Have you ever personally shorted a stock, thinking it a wise investment?"

I glanced over toward Newman, hoping to gain a nod of support. His eyes were fixed rigidly on Orr. I knew intuitively that he had already sat through a similar indoctrination of his own.

I stumbled ahead. "As you surely know, brokerage firms rarely, if ever, recommend that clients sell a stock. Platt Brothers is no different from other brokerage firms. They really only carry two ratings, buy and hold."

"Precisely," shouted Orr, pushing back his chair and jumping to his feet. "You have defined the foible of human nature that dictates why we, here, spend most of our time shorting stocks and relatively little time buying them. The cardinal rule of successful long-term investing demands that you seek value by betting against the dependable intemperance, the impatience, the madness of crowds. When stocks are wildly popular and broadly owned, they have in many instances already incorporated all of the available good news."

Orr walked over to the uncovered window and slowly lowered the blind, blocking out the errant ray. Then he continued.

"As you succinctly described, Nate, the armies and the infrastructure of our financial markets work in coalition to drive up stock prices, and they do this in violation of a fundamental principle: not all companies are winners. Some of them are fads, and some of them are frauds. And some of them simply burn to ash in the crucible of economic change."

Orr's speech was shifting into high gear. "Have you ever heard of Ponderosa System or National Chemsearch?" He did not wait for a response.

"Of course you haven't—the stocks have long since withered and the companies vanished from the face of our markets. These once darling companies were bit players in the Nifty Fifty stock market bubble of the early 1970s, a monstrosity that was heavily stoked by Wall Street promoters. The public came to believe that these special fifty companies were 'one-decision' stocks, investments that were safe to buy and hold for all time. The resulting bubble in the stock market and the inevitable crash that followed destroyed the savings and dreams and lives of small investors all over America."

"The crash hit the farm industry in Kansas, too. My dad lost his job," I offered in support of the thesis. Orr acted as if he hadn't heard my interjection.

"And the masters of Wall Street would have you believe that firms like ours, specializing in short selling, operate in a dark and sinister netherworld, that we are immoral grave dancers, sinister warlocks, and even unpatriotic!" Orr hissed as he spoke.

"I would submit that the craft we practice is about fairness, about balance, and about equilibrium. When we bet against a company's shares by selling them short, we are leaning against the stiff wind of irrational exuberance. When we are successful in deflating the share price of a puffed-up promotion like Dexter Land Company or exposing a fraud like the phony tech scheme at Sugenne Sciences—which we're working on right now—we are providing a public service by preventing these failing ventures from dragging more victims into their nets. And for this we are scorned by the establishment on Wall Street, the financial press, and even the man on the street?" Orr paced slowly across the room, returning to stand over me as I sat in the chair facing his desk.

"You see, Nate, we are the ones who wear the white hat." Orr nodded at me, shook his head up and down a couple of times as though agreeing with himself, glanced at Newman, and then gathered up a raincoat and a gray fedora, which he seemingly always wore when out of doors, and walked out of his office.

Several minutes of silence ensued. Newman and I were keenly aware of each other's presence, but neither of us uttered a sound. Finally I offered a lame comment.

"I guess I now have a better grasp of the firm's strict policy on protecting the privacy of our information. It sounds like Orr is at war with the outside world."

"Wall Street is like a sheepdog when seen from a distance— a noble and pastoral guardian, herding and maintaining order against the chaotic impulses of animal spirits." Newman spoke quietly in response to my observation. "But when seen up close, Wall Street is a dangerous pit bull, lurching against its chain and challenging encroachment. At least, this is the world according to Luc." The image of dogs and Lucas Orr seemed strangely incongruous.

"I guess you are now an official member of the fraternity. Would you like to learn our secret handshake?" Newman asked. He was joking, but he didn't smile. Still, I felt a new kinship with my colleague. I quickly recognized that promotions under Lucas Orr would not necessarily be accompanied by either increased compensation or formal documentation.

CHAPTER FOUR

By the time Cornelius Vanderbilt was in his early twenties, he operated a small fleet of sloops and schooners and had made a place for himself in the booming Hudson River trade, transporting goods and passengers. He added steamships to his growing empire and astutely deployed his vessels on routes where he might extract either the greatest operating profit or the greatest prospect of destroying his competition. He profited handsomely from his quasi-monopolies, and as his capital grew, the appendages of Vanderbilt's grasping ambition reached into markets on the upper Hudson, Long Island Sound, and the transatlantic route. When gold was discovered in California, Vanderbilt plunged headlong into the business of ferrying passengers to and from both coasts of Central America, where the hopeful prospectors would make an arduous trek across the isthmus.

As the landscape of commercial opportunity shifted, the tentacles of the Commodore's empire stretched and adapted. No longer content to merely operate businesses, he became a player in the securities of businesses operated by others. Before he ever purchased a single share of stock, Vanderbilt had already developed a canny sense for the strategy of buying and selling, a transcendent art that kept score in a realm sometimes divorced from the real world.

༄

My existence was divided into two parallel identities. Professionally, I was a soldier in Lucas Orr's battalion. We fought the forces of inequity. We raged against the folly of markets run amok. We stirred our mystical cauldron, plotting schemes of conquest. Monday through Friday, my days ran into nights. I often did not escape my office until well after midnight, trudging in silence four crosstown blocks to collapse exhausted in my Spartan, one-bedroom apartment off Times Square. The building where I lived was sandwiched between a Duane Reade pharmacy and a slender office tower that consistently advertised space for rent. Sometimes I picked up takeout on the way home from Mr. Chow's twenty-four-hour Chinese restaurant, but often I was too tired to eat.

On the weekends, I crossed the river to New Jersey, looking back in awe at the world I inhabited during the week. I had begun to feel more like an insider at work, but from Dana's neighborhood in Hoboken, I might as well have been as far away as Kansas. Removed from the immediacy of the job, I could sometimes remember the boy who had shared Bull Wertz's dreams of what Wall Street was like.

Dana had allocated me space in one of her closets, where I stored clothes for work and clothes for play. She never mentioned it, but I was aware that my inventory of garments was regularly dry-cleaned and laundered while I was away at work during the week. This little mystery found a possible explanation in something McGuire had confided to me over drinks during my last days at Platt.

"So I might as well let you know, Perk, that my keenly honed antennae have been aware for some time that you have been fornicating with the delicious young Dana Rocca." He raised his nearly empty tumbler to toast me.

"No worries, my friend—your secret is safe with me," he added with a wink, having efficiently confirmed his suspicion by my crimson silence. "Here's what you don't know." McGuire glanced around the near-empty pub as if to confirm that no one was eavesdropping. "This darling that you lie with is not just any rookie research analyst." He paused for effect, and I felt naked in the silence.

McGuire continued in a hushed voice, "Dana Rocca is actually Dana Rockefeller. It's my guess that she is testing herself, to see if she can make it on her own. I saw a letter written on the Rockefeller office stationary sitting on her desk. And once I saw her dropped off in a chauffeured limousine, blocks from the building; she got out and walked the rest of the way."

McGuire's skillfully delivered barbs always left his targets wondering about the veracity of his tales. I wasn't sure whether he was ribbing me, but I had no intention of embarrassing myself any further by asking him.

"I have to congratulate you," McGuire had said. You went fishing for love, and gold came up on the line."

When I studied the neat display of my freshly cleaned clothes and the neatly hung shirts, ironed as I liked them with extra starch, I wondered whether the family chauffeur from Dana's "real" life was escorting my laundry to the Lexington

Avenue dry cleaner when he drove Dana back and forth across the river. I had decided not to ask Dana about McGuire's tale because I didn't really want to know the answer. Perhaps Dana was the girl I had dreamed I would meet when I came to New York—someone from a simple background like my own, with ambition, intelligence, and beauty. But it was also possible that she was the kind of girl I would never have dared to imagine— an heiress from one of the great American families. McGuire had infected my mind with the thought of unimaginable wealth and power; I was afraid that the resolution of the truth of Dana's heritage might end up sullying my original quaint ideal and disturbing the romance between us. So I reveled in my ignorance even as I occasionally poked here and there for any evidence that might confirm his astonishing claim.

Our Saturday routine was predictable. We would usually sleep in until eight and then go for a jog along the waterfront, a landscape of shuttered factories with broken windows and crumbling piers.

Hoboken was known as the "mile square city," its grid of neatly arrayed blocks lying in marshy lands across the Hudson River from lower Manhattan. The city had served as a bustling port for much of the eighteenth and early part of the nineteenth century, until the archetypal port town had become obsolete with the advent of national highways, containerization, and mega shipping ports. At the outbreak of World War I, the federal government had taken over the downtown Hamburg-American line terminals and used the city as the primary port of embarkation for three million U.S. soldiers. The dreams of the troops for an early return immortalized the small burg in the memorable slogan, "Heaven, Hell, or Hoboken!"

The aroma of a Maxwell House coffee plant on the north end of town lent an enticing aura to one crisp fall morning as I jogged in the company of the woman who stirred me at night and made me laugh and wonder during the day.

"It seems unfathomable that all of this great real estate just sits here idle..." she said aloud during the morning jaunt. "And with these amazing views across the water to Manhattan!"

I glanced beyond the wind-whipped waters of the Hudson River and thought for a moment that I spied the dark silhouette of my Park Avenue office building. But then it ducked away out of view behind another looming tower closer to the shore.

"Just imagine," Dana proclaimed, with a broad sweep of her hand, "a resident of Hoboken gets to look at the skyline of Manhattan, while a resident of Manhattan looks at the abandoned brown fields of Hoboken, New Jersey. Mark my words...the land we stand upon will be very valuable someday."

Dana spoke with the crisp authority of a Wall Street analyst, but I wondered whether she possessed the Rockefeller talent for spotting good real estate. It was hard to figure out which it might be from her appearance. Her daily work uniform could have come from the Gap—or Prada. It was simple, consistent, and so effortlessly elegant that it was impossible to tell what anything had cost, with the notable exception of her trademark Cartier watch with the red alligator band. She almost always wore a crisp white men's shirt with a dark pantsuit, a classic double strand of pearls, that Cartier watch, and one of her varied assortment of boutique shoes. On the weekends when we were together, she looked barely different—more casual, but still classic, with her blue eyes, rich golden skin, slightly crooked mouth, and a low ponytail gathering up a bouquet of shiny brown hair. This was a woman who did not need makeup or fine clothes to establish her personality. She might have been an heiress or just another hopeful Wall Street analyst, but either way, she carried herself with such confidence and nonchalant aloofness that she emanated the aura of one who was more than just an ordinary beautiful young woman.

After our jog we would stop for lunch, either at a streetside café or at Lisa's Deli, where sausages hung in links from the ceiling and men behind the counter chattered in Italian while filling orders.

One day, while we were feasting on a matched pair of oversized subs swimming with hot peppers, Dana asked me the question I had been hoping to avoid.

"Nate? What is Lucas Orr really like?"

I paused, trying to come up with a response that would short-circuit the conversation.

"Well, you know, he is incredibly dedicated to his work."

"Um-umh," she said. "And?"

"We all work very hard to generate great investment ideas, and he is the leader of this effort." I realized immediately that my half-truth served to convey enough information to end the conversation.

"So, that's the way it's going to be?" Dana cut through my obfuscation with alacrity. "This amazing job, which you owe to the brilliance of an idea that I laid in your lap, is now *off-limits* for conversation?" Dana arched her eyebrows.

"What's new at Platt?" I inquired, redirecting the conversation. Dana stood and kissed me on the forehead.

"That's okay. You can keep your secrets. I, of course, have mysteries of my own." I decided that if she was going to leave it at that, I did indeed love her. She grinned as if to indicate that she was aware of the rumors regarding her aristocratic pedigree.

"What I will tell you is that Everest Cullman asked me to drop my coverage of the chemical industry and pick up coverage of the semiconductor stocks. He said I am far too great a talent to be trolling through the wasteland of Port Arthur, Texas. It's kind of strange, because I never got the impression that he was paying particularly close attention to my work."

"Everyone pays close attention to you," I teased.

Ignoring my jocularity, Dana continued, "He actually mentioned something about having received compliments from clients that lead me to believe that my change in coverage wasn't even his own idea. In any case, there is a ton of innovation coming in Silicon Valley, so this is my own big chance to plunge into the excitement of the unknown." It occurred to me that Lucas Orr had poached the wrong talent from Platt Brothers.

"In other news, your old boss, Gil Tanser, was sent to purgatory *downtown*. It seems that he was sleeping with one of the sales assistants fresh out of college. The girl's father found out about it and showed up in the lobby of Platt's office building asking to see Tanser." Dana chuckled.

"The girl's father was apparently a retired detective in the NYPD. He talked his way past the elevator security before making his way upstairs, where he politely called on Mr. Tanser. When Gil came out, the father drew a handgun, waved it threateningly, and told him to leave his daughter alone. The receptionist saw the whole thing. Evidently Tanser melted under the threat when the girl's dad said something like, 'Listen, buster, I know where you live. You even talk to my little girl again, and you're gonna be looking behind you every step you take.' Naturally, the receptionist called security when she saw the gun, and all hell broke loose. Can you imagine a gun on the trading floor?"

"Well, actually, no." My mind pulled me back to my own office, where violence was expressed in dollars and cents.

"As you can imagine, that created quite a story around the firm for at least two or three days, and it neatly ended Tanser's career," Dana continued.

"Genghis...gone downtown!" I had a hard time imagining the sales and trading floors at Platt without the looming presence of Tanser.

"Yeah, well, they've already found a replacement to crack the whip over the galley slaves," Dana said. "It's no more fun on your old floor than it was when Tanser was stalking the aisles."

"Downtown" referred to a suite of offices that Platt maintained for its most prominent retired partners. The space was located in a slightly lower rent district a mere ten blocks south of the main office, but downtown was a world removed from the front row of the capital markets. I had been there once to deliver a package to the firm's former chairman. Downtown was a bleak gallery of former titans and their secretaries—sometimes women who had worked for them for decades—where the phones rarely rang. The place was muted, except on the days when there was a fluttering of excitement and straightening of ties before the fossilized financiers trooped uptown to the Platt headquarters for the quarterly business update. To be sent downtown was to join a repository of men in fine attire who wandered aimlessly through an arcade of fancy rolltop desks and deal mementos, attending to their philanthropic activities and telling each other stories about "the old days."

"You might also be interested to hear that the trading desk took a bath on a proprietary trading position in some piece of garbage called Sugenne Sciences," Dana added. "The company's CEO resigned, and the SEC is investigating accounting fraud. The shares dropped like a stone, thirty points, when the news was announced." Dana looked at me in a way that made me feel ashamed. I wondered if she suspected that Tantalus had prospered at the expense of her employer.

"Uh, yeah, that trade sounds familiar," I said. Platt's misfortune had represented new gold coined in the realm of Tantalus.

"And on the back of dismal all-around business results, I heard the firm will be announcing another round of layoffs soon. It seems like Platt Brothers has developed a run of bad luck since you left." I was feeling sorry that I had asked for an update on the old firm.

Over the next month, I barely saw Orr in the office. I had come to understand that these periods of extended leave were known as "Orr gone hunting." No one seemed to have any real idea where he was or what he was doing during these absences, but invariably a new influx of profits would flow into the firm soon after he returned. During one of these periods when Orr was cryptically away from the office, I spotted him entering a dark sedan at the curbside of our building as I was returning from an afternoon coffee run. As I stopped to watch him slide into the backseat of the vehicle, I momentarily caught the brown-eyed gaze of a beautiful woman seated inside the vehicle. Then the door shut quickly, and they were gone.

Later that week, when Newman and I had wandered off to have an outdoor lunch at our spot on Bryant Park, I asked him for some guidance on how he thought about and managed the conflict between his professional and private lives.

"I mean, would you tell your girlfriend what sorts of things you were working on—if you felt that you could really trust her?" I asked.

A perceptible blush crossed Newman's pale complexion, and he quickly looked away. I knew in an instant that my question had been awkward. In an attempt to recover, I continued.

"I mean hypothetically, would you tell someone that you were really close to?"

Newman turned back, fixing his eyes on me implacably. His skin had reassumed its nondescript coloring.

"You know what the firm's policy says. There isn't any ambiguity there."

༄

The first big kill at Tantalus in which I played a small role culminated on a hot day in midsummer. It scored untold millions in profits for the firm, and it reinforced my faith in the brilliance of my enigmatic mentor. For two years, Orr had been tracking the meteoric rise of a Florida company called Marlin Networks. When Marlin had first issued stock in an initial public offering at twelve dollars per share, 250,000 subscribers used the company's Internet access service. From that humble beginning, the company had successfully built a unique community, a walled garden amidst the chaos of the surging new global Internet, where its customers could shop, socialize, and otherwise entertain themselves with a few clicks of a mouse and a computer keyboard. The number of subscribers to Marlin's service had exploded upward to five million, and the stock had followed, trading in the eighty-dollar range.

But Orr had concluded that the financial foundation of Marlin was constructed on quicksand. The company's robust growth rate in subscribers had been built on an extensive and costly consumer marketing campaign that included carpet-bombing millions of U.S. households with free copies of the disk required to launch the service. Simple math indicated that it cost the company about a hundred and twenty dollars in total marketing costs to acquire each new subscriber. These large expenses were easily managed when competition was scant, subscriber rolls were growing quickly, and users continued to be charged their ten-dollar subscriber fee each month. Customers who were retained for one year essentially repaid the cost of their initial acquisition, so the key to the company's financial health was keeping customers from churning out and canceling the service.

Orr, assisted by a team of number crunchers, including me, had deciphered the financial levers likely to drive the success or failure of Marlin Networks, boiling the investment challenge down to an accurate prediction of subscriber attrition.

"Two years ago we began tracking one thousand unique, randomly selected users of Marlin Networks that we plucked from the social networking rooms of the service," Orr explained. "People like MetsFan22, FoxyGurl...you get the idea." I could tell that he was enjoying the eulogy.

"Using this sample of users, I have gained a fairly scientific approximation of user stickiness. We have now spied into the lives of these faceless people for twenty-four months, and we have meticulously tracked the rate at which some of them simply drop out of the user directory and evaporate into the mist." Lucas Orr broke into one of his rare grins. I noticed that he had nearly imperceptible dimples.

"As a result of this analysis, I am now prepared to declare with confidence that growth has peaked for this house of cards, and a world of pain lies ahead because subscriber churn has spiked. We're shorting the stock in size."

My first reaction had been to wonder about Orr's invincibility. There were already many vocal bears on the company, and these naysayers had been trampled underfoot as the stock had risen to heights far beyond anyone's rational imagination. As if reading my mind, Orr explained his cool resolution.

"Here is the difference between Tantalus and a run-of-the-mill short seller. They are merely guessing, whereas I will not act until I am certain that I have broken the code." Orr was almost preening as he described his own genius. I was wondering whether he might also possess critical information that he had not shared with me.

"I see," I offered up lamely while slowly scratching my chin. Newman had instructed me that this gesture was scientifically proven to subliminally suggest high intellect to an observer. Newman winked at me.

The Golden Dog

"Bye-bye, Marlin," he sang.

Within three weeks, Marlin Networks issued a grim financial update. The stock fell forty points in a single trading session. Orr was wearing the white hat, and I was feeling grand about my new career.

It was an unspoken rule at Tantalus that there was to be no celebration, no gloating, and no chest-thumping when investments paid off in a big way. Instead, after the firm monetized a large gain, there was an expectation that every employee should feel even greater pressure to perform. There were two reasons for that silent dictum. Unlike most firms, which gave out bonuses once a year at a prescribed time, Orr provided bonuses to his top team when he completed a big deal. The awards were in the form of "points," which entitled the recipient to a certain ownership stake in the funds we managed. That meant that I was considerably richer after the Marlin deal than I had been before, even if this wealth was all on paper. The bonus points Orr handed me were no longer in the five-digit range; my bonus for this deal alone had jumped an entire digit in a matter of months. But despite the sudden arrival of personal prosperity, I felt strangely desensitized to my good fortune. And I suppose this was Orr's intent.

The hunt continued; the growing capital pool needed to be redeployed with each big win, and we had to produce new ideas. As I went about my daily investigatory tasks in a smallish private office down the hall from the seat of the master, I was feeling a swelling obligation to contribute. I felt I owed it to Orr. Each day that I hit a dead end in my quest for the next bonanza, I could feel it. When I walked through the reception area, I increasingly sensed that the ebony-faced African masks were glowering at me in disappointment.

CHAPTER FIVE

Emboldened by his growing financial success and consumed by an unyielding quest, the Staten Island farm boy who made good became a fearless man operating against a hostile world. No challenge was too daunting, no competitor unassailable. The Commodore soon became famous for his ferocious attacks on established competitors, sometimes establishing brutally below-market pricing, designed principally to extort a generous payoff for him to go away.

Cornelius Vanderbilt's public persona combined the aura of respectable commercial eminence with the swagger and profanity of a dockside boat-hand, a unique new blend that defined an emerging class of American moguls. The hardscrabble tycoon owed nothing to title or birthright. Everything he possessed was an outgrowth of his voracious appetite for success and the disciplined practice of a newly respectable craft: speculation. The generations of colorful rogues of finance and industry who would follow in Vanderbilt's footsteps developed a modern decorum and vernacular, but at their core, nothing had really changed.

∽

One Friday evening in the early fall, Dana and I coordinated an early departure from New York in a pouring rainstorm. She was standing on a mutually agreed street corner under the cover of an overhanging canopy to a shop entrance, staring at the new fashions of the season in the store, when I rushed up and embraced her from behind.

"Quick, we need to get out of here immediately. Orr's people are tailing me!" Dana looked startled for an instant before she realized that I was only joking. I briefly wondered why she had been fooled for even a second, but in a moment, I was back in the pleasure of the wet night as we splashed playfully through puddles, covering ourselves with one shared umbrella as we navigated our escape. Commuting times during bad weather in New York were twice as long as normal, so by the time we arrived in Hoboken my socks were wet and I was looking forward to a hot shower and a cold beer.

We stepped into the vestibule of Dana's apartment just as a figure sprinted up with a delivery of dry cleaning. Visible under the plastic wrap in his hands was my favorite business shirt, a dark blue pinpoint oxford with a white collar, dangling neatly on the outside hanger of his handful of garments.

"Delivery for Dana Rocca?" I inquired matter-of-factly. "I can take that from you," I said, reaching out for the exchange. The deliveryman had been hunched over to protect his face from the rain and recoiled in a defensive posture as I reached forward. He looked at me suspiciously, but when his eyes lit on Dana, he broke into a broad grin.

"Hey, Dana. So this is the guy? You sure managed to keep him under wraps for a heck of a long time," he said.

Then, turning to me, he said, "We usually just hang the stuff on the hook here in the vestibule." He was a man of perhaps thirty, with jet-black hair slicked back, a handsome olive complexion, and a deep voice. Despite his coloring, his eyes were the same blue as Dana's. I immediately introduced myself as Dana's boyfriend.

"Hey, great to meet you, Nate," he said and extended a crushing handshake. "I'm Dana's cousin, Joe Rocca. We have a dry-cleaning shop just down the road in Jersey City. Take care of Dana's cleaning on a complimentary basis. You know, she's just getting started and all."

I was momentarily disoriented by the introduction.

"Dana kept sending us this guy's clothes, but she never gave me any of the details. C'mon, kiddo," he said to Dana, "why don't you bring him to Aunt Maria's lunch on Sunday. Let the family look him over. We can keep this living together thing just between us." He winked at me.

"You oughta come," Joe continued. "You won't go away hungry." Then looking around he said, "Sorry, gotta run; the van is double-parked," and he was gone as quickly as he had appeared. Dana grabbed the dry cleaning and bolted up the stairs ahead of me.

After securing the deadbolt and chain to her apartment door, Dana turned to face me. We studied each other for several long seconds without speaking.

"So. Now you've met my cousin, you can figure out for yourself that the Rockefeller rumors are nothing but a gag," Dana said. I couldn't tell if her tone had a hint of bitterness, or if she was just being direct.

"How did you know?" I asked, shocked and embarrassed that she knew what I was thinking.

"McGuire had been dropping hints about my fancy family. At the office Christmas party he was, not surprisingly, skunk-drunk. You might also remember having skipped out on attending the party due to a stomach bug, leaving me exposed to all manner of strange solicitation." Wall Street holiday festivities were notorious for bringing out the worst in people.

Dana continued, "So I asked him what he was always kidding me about. He told me in his smarmy way that he knew my 'big secret.' At first I thought he was talking about us. Then he laid it on me about my 'assumed identity.'" I was imagining McGuire slobbering over Dana in some dark corner of a cavernous restaurant as, all around them, middle-aged men made fools of themselves, dancing to the blaring beat of teenage music.

"I couldn't believe it. I thought he was kidding, but he was serious. So I asked, 'How many people know about this?' 'The whole effing floor,' he says and gives one of those belly laughs. So I decided to play along. I denied it vociferously and angrily, which made him even surer that I was Ms. Rockefeller in disguise. I thought, what the heck, can't do me any harm. I've been wondering if you swallowed the story."

"Yes and no," I offered sheepishly. "Of course, I didn't care one way or another," I said, grabbing her hands and eyeing her affectionately. "Truth be told, there is something about you that has the scent of privilege. It seemed possible."

"Well, it couldn't be less true," Dana said, and she told me her story. I was embarrassed by the realization of how little either of us knew about each other's past lives. I didn't even know that she was an orphan. Her parents had died when she was thirteen, and she moved in with her older sister and her husband in Philadelphia. One of her teachers picked her out as a star student and encouraged her to apply for a scholarship at an elite boarding school, where she was accepted with a full ride. Next came a scholarship to Princeton and, after that, Stanford Business School, and she emerged from this schooling with top marks and without a single dollar of tuition debt. While she was living in these privileged environments, she had studied the other girls and emulated the ones she admired. She copied their style so successfully that when she said she came from Philadelphia, people assumed she was a member of one of the old Main Line families.

"Of course, the Philadelphians weren't fooled," she added. "Not that I was trying. But anyway, if you don't have a street named after your ancestors, you're considered a newcomer down there, and of course there is no one, but absolutely no one in that crowd with a name like Rocca.

"My aunts and uncles and cousins and my sister and her husband really made it possible. They don't have much, but whenever I've needed something, they've been there for me.

85

But I have also learned what it's like to live on life's top floor from the people I went to school with, and I've always worked hard to fit in and make something better of myself.

"So do you still love me now that you know I'm a Rocca, not a Rocca-feller?" Dana asked the question flippantly, but I had the sense that she really wanted to hear my reassurance. Perhaps she was worried that she had let my delusion last too long. I grabbed her in a tight embrace, burying my face in the soft fold of her neck, which was faintly scented with a pleasant perfume.

"Anyway," she said finally pulling away, "perhaps it is time for you to meet some of the crazed Rocca clan—that is if you are still interested. How would you like to accept Joe's invitation and come to Sunday dinner at Aunt Maria's?"

At the appointed time on Sunday, Joe arrived to ferry us the short ride to Aunt Maria's row house on a residential side street of West New York, a New Jersey town with glimpses of the New York skyline.

"Us Roccas are close, just not too close," Joe blurted. "You can see we need to live in different towns—separated by all of one or two miles."

We parked at the curb in front of an aging, two-story stucco home with brown trim after Joe removed an orange cone, which had been protecting our parking spot. A small, white statue of the Virgin sat to one side of a stone walkway leading to the house. Dana took a deep breath as she approached the house.

Two older men in white shirts, who were sitting on the front porch, stood when they saw Dana and smiled. Suddenly the warmth of their reunion moment was shattered by the blare of a car radio nearby. One of the older men, an imposing physical presence with a small paunch, sprinted past us and stood in the middle of the street, eyeing the offending car as it approached. Suddenly the car radio went silent as the older man growled, "Not in my neighborhood you don't." Then a torrent of Italian poured from his lips as a group of stunned teenagers in the car sat motionless. In a moment the man was back, embracing Dana—a model of avuncular affection.

"Shame on you. Living so close, and yet ignoring your Uncle Frank for so long." Frank held Dana's cheeks between the caress of two strong hands and studied her closely. "So much like your father," he said before smothering her in a suffocating embrace. Thumping Joe on the back, Frank turned and walked back to the house without acknowledging me. I turned to face Dana with an inquisitive look.

"Not outside—he wants to meet you inside the house," Dana whispered with a shrug. The second man who had been sitting on the porch, older than Frank and with thin wisps of white hair, had also retreated inside, and we followed them. An eruption of hugs and tears greeted Dana the moment she crossed the transom. When she was able to untangle herself from the embrace of aunts and cousins and nephews and nieces, Dana turned toward me with a sweep of her hands.

"I would like everyone to meet my boyfriend, Nate," she said proudly. "He also works in New York City."

"Nate who? What's your last name?" blurted the man with the wisps of white hair. The frail and tottering interrogator had not been introduced, but I gathered that he had earned a certain deference.

"Nate Perkins," Dana replied confidently. Frank shook my hand with the bruising clasp that seemed to be a Rocca family trait, and then he escorted me through a narrow hallway dripping with the pleasing scent of garlic and simmering meat. Stepping through a screen door in the rear of the house that opened into a narrow strip of backyard, Frank applied a firm kick of his soft-soled black shoe to the rump of a white and black dog that sat at the foot of a short stairway. The mutt, unsurprised at the offense, ambled off to a corner of the yard where two youngsters were playing.

Joe, who had been walking alongside me, whispered into my ear, "He does that just to remind the dog who's boss."

A bottle of beer, dripping with beads of cold moisture, was thrust into my hand as Frank, Joe, and the white-haired man convened in a small circle of lawn chairs around me.

"So, you're in the banking business?" Frank asked.

Almost simultaneously, the white-haired man interrupted. "You a churchgoer, Nate?" I looked back and forth between the two men before responding.

"Well, not banking, really—I am in the investing business."

"Oh, stock market, huh? Well, how about a stock tip for your friend Frank? You can trust us to keep it all in the family." He leaned forward in his chair, his blue eyes popping and the muscles in his neck bulging. Three pair of eyes studied me with avaricious intent as I shifted uncomfortably in my seat. I couldn't even imagine what Lucas Orr would think of this spectacle and of my cross-examination. I was so close to the spires of Manhattan, and yet I was sitting in the midst of a scene from a bygone time. Suddenly Dana burst out of the back door, and the door slammed behind her. Seeing our private parley, she rushed to my rescue.

"Let me guess, Uncle Frank is badgering you for stock tips? Sorry to interrupt, but it's time for dinner."

We trooped into the house, where I was assigned a seat between Joe and the white-haired man, while Dana sat across from me. Over the next two hours, we basked in the warmth of a boisterous family over endless helpings of homemade food. For the most part, Frank led the conversation, regaling us with humorous tales of everyday life that he collected in his gift shop down on Kennedy Boulevard. It wasn't easy for me to match his blunt physicality with the image of a man selling birthday cards and scented candles. After multiple bottles of Chianti had been consumed, Frank turned his attention to Dana.

"We haven't seen you at Mass for several months." His brow was furled, and the late-day shadow of his beard created a threatening effect as he locked eyes on his prodigal niece. "You know that I swore an oath to your father that I would always look out for his little girl."

Dana looked at Frank impassively as Aunt Maria, who had been shuttling back and forth to the kitchen for most of the evening, blurted out, "That's enough, Frank. We are not going to talk about that again."

"What?" Frank exclaimed, pushing back his chair from the table and appealing to a general sympathy as he stretched out his arms and shrugged his shoulders. "My young niece troops off to some strange profession on the sordid streets of the faceless city, and I cannot be there for her to help her wrestle with the important issues of conscience." Frank looked at me, leaving the impression that he suspected that I was either sordid, without conscience, or perhaps both.

"Okay, this has been a lovely evening," Dana said and stood, indicating to Joe that it was time to leave. "Nate and I really need to be getting back. Our morning labors begin very early, just like work in the old country."

We were silent during the car ride back to Hoboken. When we reached Dana's building, she embraced Joe with sincere affection before alighting from the car.

That night, as we turned in for bed, Dana said, "Now you know the whole story. Sure, I love my family, but I would rather die than live in their world." I nodded sympathetically.

"You have to understand, Nate—I would do anything to avoid that fate." Then Dana rolled over. As she was falling asleep, I heard her say to herself, "*Anything.*"

CHAPTER SIX

As he neared the age of sixty, with a fortune of over ten million dollars safely invested in a diverse pool of secure assets, Cornelius Vanderbilt decided to hold a celebration. The destination was to be the old world of Europe, and the means of transport would be his very own ship, the North Star, at 275 feet long and 2,500 tons, the largest steamship in the world and a marvel of nautical engineering. But what truly distinguished the vessel was its spectacular internal beauty. Staterooms were appointed with the finest furnishings and fabrics while murals of famous people adorned the ceilings of the ship's dazzling dining room. Vanderbilt had constructed a floating palace for himself. The grand tour was not intended as an opportunity to fawn at the cultural offerings of Europe's grand society. His purpose was quite different—to place on prominent international display the stark commercial achievements of America's leading self-made businessman.

During the course of the Commodore's fifty-eight-day journey to England, the Baltic, and on to Russia, he received the news that one of his affiliated companies had ceased making payments to Vanderbilt's agent. Although Vanderbilt had sold most of his stock ownership in the business, he had continued to receive a rich commission that totaled 20 percent of gross receipts. A messy legal wrangle was expected. But the Commodore had a different idea. Penning a brief open letter that was published in the dailies upon his return to America, Vanderbilt announced to his adversaries, "Gentlemen: You have undertaken to cheat me. I won't sue you, for the law is too slow. I'll ruin you. Yours truly, Cornelius Vanderbilt."

The Golden Dog

It was early December when I noticed Newman and Orr engaged in a prolonged, closed-door meeting that lasted well over an hour. To say this was unusual would be an understatement; the typical audience any employee of the firm had with Lucas Orr was usually over in ten minutes. At length, my intercom buzzed and Orr barked a command to enter his office. When I pushed the door open and crossed the threshold, I noticed Newman sunk down on the leather sofa.

"Sit," Orr instructed.

I lowered myself into one of the armchairs that flanked Orr's desk. "We have a somewhat delicate project here that Newman and I agree is well suited for you to lead." He paused. My initial trepidation at being summoned melted away. I puffed out my chest imperceptibly and raised my eyebrows, awaiting Orr's command.

"Really. Okay, great." I didn't know what else to say.

"Ted here has a *friend* in the business who has put his firm in an untenable situation, and that firm is now sitting on a bomb." Orr accented the word *friend* with obvious intent. I knew what he meant.

"We are going to light the fuse. Plot out the specifics with Newman, and keep me in the loop." Orr turned away in his chair, and the meeting was over.

92

I followed Newman into his office next to mine, one door closer to the master. His shoulders drooped as he walked, making him appear even shorter than his slight five-foot-six frame. He shut the door securely behind us, and when he began to speak, he did not look at me directly.

"There is a guy I know from Yale named Vinod Sharma. We used to be pretty close, but we hadn't seen much of each other until I met up with him about a week ago. He is one of the senior guys at Highstone Partners, the hedge fund." He stopped and stared at his feet.

"Highstone? Have you noticed how these firms all seem to be named after animals of prey or words that represent strength or durability?" I remarked. Newman did not offer a hint of interest in my observation. His mind was focused elsewhere.

I was familiar with Highstone. The firm's founder was Munson Erlich, a young whiz kid who had graduated from one of Wall Street's storied arbitrage desks. Erlich had hung out his own shingle after a couple of banner compensation years and had quickly gathered up an investing kitty of several hundred million dollars from a distinguished list of endowments and foundations. Engaging in a broad swath of strategies, including stocks, bonds, and derivatives, Highstone had run up some early success, further enhancing Erlich's reputation and boosting his ability to raise funds. Having witnessed Highstone from my perch at Platt Brothers, however, I was dubious of the savvy of the highly touted firm. Highstone had been one of the most aggressive hedge funds in badgering underwriters for allocations of hot IPOs—initial public offerings—a performance-enhancing gift that underwriters were able to dole out to their favored clients. I had no idea where Newman's conversation was leading, so I remained quiet.

"Owing to my friend Sharma's efforts, Highstone has purchased 18 percent of the stock of National Airways, though this fact is not yet known publicly. I had dinner with Sharma a couple of weeks ago, and he confided that he is feeling pretty nervous about the outlook for National Airways, with oil prices going up and passenger traffic trending down." Newman spoke as if he were directing a biology class in the dissection of a frog.

"To complicate matters—for him, that is—Sharma is incredibly concerned about his standing within the firm. The partners at Highstone eat what they kill. He has not generated any green this year and, apparently, the overall fund has seen its performance slipping. Several of Highstone's largest investors are threatening to put in redemption notices, asking for their money back, and the firm is very much on edge. If National Airways blows up, it will turn his partners against him in the most savage way."

But we will get there first, I thought to myself, and I had the sense that the executioner's axe was being placed in my hands. Newman continued his dispassionate presentation.

"We have done our work, and Sharma's concerns are well placed. National operates with a dwindling financial margin of safety, and he is right that the recent spike in fuel prices combined with a turndown in air travel will likely push the company into losses. In the last two days, Orr has shorted more than two million shares of National Airways."

The life had been draining slowly from Newman's presentation when he finally turned to face me. His final instructions were delivered forcefully but with undertones of a feeble apology.

"Your assignment is to push Sharma over the brink. Convince him to capitulate and to puke his oversized position into the marketplace. We will cover our position in the chaos that ensues." His rendering of the plan seemed clinically detached, but when he was finished talking, he swept his hand in the air vaguely and said, "I'm sorry; I need some privacy now. Good luck on your assignment. Orr is counting on you."

And with those words, I was flung out into the night alone, to inflict torment for the greater glory of the Tantalus Fund.

After a handful of back-and-forth calls, I connected with Kent Toothman, the airline analyst at Platt Brothers. Toothman was an empty suit, full of boast and babble and distinctly clueless in the art of picking stocks. He was the source of local legend, still retold in snickers by the veterans at Platt Brothers. Years ago, a young trainee in the investment banking department had tossed a handful of oversized presentation books from a private client meeting into an airport garbage can instead of carting them back to the office for disposal following the session. The books, clearly marked "Confidential" in bold letters, were recovered by an airport custodian and ultimately mailed back to Platt Brothers headquarters—after enough time had passed that they had likely been perused by untold numbers of prying eyes. The foolish trainee who couldn't bother to carry a heavy bag for the return trip was given a brutal reprimand, and his job was spared only through the intercession of his father, a well-regarded retired former partner. That trainee was Kent Toothman, who was subsequently shuffled off to the research department where it was assumed he could do little damage covering the airline stocks. Toothman was damaged merchandise, but he was just right for my assignment.

"Uh, Kent, this is Nate Perkins...over here at Lucas Orr's shop."

"Perkins...oh, Perkins! How the heck are ya? Quite a coup, landing that job right off the sales desk. What can I do for you?"

I had the impression that Toothman was gritting his teeth, having to deal with young Nate Perkins, now the important customer.

"We're doing some work on airline stocks over here, and I was hoping you could pull together a very select dinner with the biggest holders of the shares—just a small handful of guys—so we can brainstorm together over a nice meal and some good wine." I tried to make it sound like a request although we both knew that I expected nothing less than respectful compliance.

"Hey, great idea," blurted Toothman. "I had been thinking the same thing. We'll do it right here in one of our private dining rooms. Let me get back to you with a date."

"Great, Kent—good. Just do me a favor and give me a call when you put together a guest list; I might have an idea for a name or two." I couldn't take the risk that Sharma would not be in attendance. And with that single phone call, the trap was sprung. I was certain that the distressed Mr. Sharma would accept the now certain invitation.

When the night arrived, I was pleased to note that in addition to Toothman, Sharma, and myself, the dinner included only three other attendees. Toothman was a lanky, goofy-looking guy with unruly brown hair speckled with gray. Sharma sported a garish red paisley tie, as if the ebullience of his garb could disguise his misery. He was excessively friendly to everyone assembled around a handsome wood table in one of the handful of elegant small dining rooms in the Platt Brothers executive suite. A pale-faced waiter dressed in all black hovered over our gathering, his nose tilted slightly in the air as if to reassure us that he wasn't listening.

As the dinner proceeded I became increasingly aware that I was being watched. One of the attendees, who had bobbed his head up and down repeatedly when he had introduced himself as Duncan Bridges of Bridges Capital, seemed more interested in observing me than in any other aspect of the event. He was a tall, straight-backed fellow of perhaps fifty, with pink cheeks and a bird's nest of curly salt-and-pepper hair. Since he did not appear to be particularly threatening, I smiled in his direction on the several occasions when our eyes met. The two other investors in attendance were relatively junior analysts representing very large firms, who seemed content to remain silent, unobtrusively transcribing notes from the conversation.

Toothman was mating with his fourth glass of merlot as I launched into my soliloquy.

"We have been interested in the value story with these airlines," I offered, hinting a positive bias. "The aircraft alone, in the case of many of the stocks, are worth the entire market value, meaning you are paying practically nothing for the ongoing franchise." Sharma's demeanor perked up instantly, and Toothman briefly raised his nostrils above the circumference of his wine goblet. And then I brought the pendulum back down.

"But here is our *issue*." I emphasized the last word with meaning as I passed around copies of a single sheet of paper, cluttered with numbers.

"We have tracked the financial metrics of each major airline going back for ten years. The key driver for earnings is what they call net yield, calculated as the profit earned per available seat mile." Sharma shifted uncomfortably as he studied the document I had presented. Toothman craned his neck to examine the evidence I had unveiled. The two unseasoned researchers were scribbling furiously.

"And it has become exceedingly clear to us that the earnings projections for all airline stocks are far in excess of what is likely to be achieved, given the recent inputs to our earnings models."

When I noticed that Sharma was raising a finger as if to enter an objection, I quickly interjected. "And here is the clincher." I noticed that our tuxedoed attendant, clearing used silverware at the end of the table, turned his head ever so slightly to have an open ear positioned in the direction of my coup de grace.

"We spoke to the CFO of National Airways just yesterday," I said, and I saw Vinod Sharma freeze.

"And without admitting it directly, during our aggressive interrogation, he indicated that the coming quarters are going to be extremely challenging from an earnings perspective." I briefly pondered what threats or inducements Lucas Orr had employed to convince the critical financial staffer to roll over for us and confess a weak financial outlook.

"So, what do you guys think?" I leaned back in my chair, spreading my arms in victory, and summoned the waiter for a glass of the nectar that had, by then, taken command of Kent Toothman's mind.

Duncan Bridges, who had mostly interjected a few pleasantly phrased questions until that point in the evening, spoke.

"It appears that you've nailed it. These stocks are broken and likely headed much lower."

Toothman suddenly looked up as if roused from a deep slumber. The two neophytes immediately looked toward Sharma, who quickly rose from the table. He spoke with a pleasant hint of British, but his cadence was unsteady. A single small bead of sweat clung perilously to his forehead at the hairline. He held his head rigidly to prevent the telltale marker from shaking loose.

"This has been a fascinating evening. And now I bid you all good evening," he said. With that, a beaten man walked out into the night.

Brief pleasantries were exchanged between the five of us who remained. Duncan Bridges approached me, guiding me by the elbow to a spot by the window apart from the others, where we could see the twinkling lights of Broadway below. He gripped my hand and shook it vigorously, his head bobbing like a barnyard rooster.

"The name is Duncan Bridges, and my firm is Bridges Capital." Since he had previously introduced himself at the commencement of the evening, I suspected that he had more to say.

"An inspired performance," he offered. We were standing close enough that I could see a faded stain on the yellow and blue striped club tie, which hung loosely at his neck. "I'm sure you know that Highstone is loaded to the gills with airline stocks. Going for the kill, eh?" He was staring at me with the informed look of a Wall Street veteran, someone who had done his time in the trenches. He thrust a business card into my hand.

"Call me, or even better, come visit me. I'd enjoy talking stocks with you. You obviously have a talent for this game. I've been around the block a few times—you might even find I could add a little objective advice when things get hairy." My first inclination was to embrace his seemingly genuine offer of friendship, especially given the growing sense of isolation

I was feeling in my job. But I also knew that Orr's policy unambiguously discouraged this sort of outside networking. Conflicted, I nodded, thanked him without commitment while pocketing his card, and turned to complete my final task of the evening.

Ambling over toward Toothman, who was standing with his back up against a delicate mahogany table with my handout loosely clenched in his fingers, I offered up an idea.

"If you want to leverage off this meeting, to make your own research call on the stocks, that would be fine," I whispered so that the others could not hear. Toothman, momentarily startled by my approach, shifted quickly on his feet. In the process his arm swung erratically to one side, striking violently against a gilded table clock that had likely occupied its place unmolested for many years. The clock crashed destructively against hard wood as broken glass and cracked plaster sprayed away from the point of impact. The others in the room turned to see what had caused the commotion as Toothman stepped decisively away from the scene of the mishap, making no effort to recover the clock.

"No worries, just the gong going off on our evening together," said Toothman, demonstrating the quick repartee of an accident-prone entertainer. Turning back to face me, Toothman greedily pocketed the copy of my analytical dissection, and a smile crossed his parched lips, which had turned a vinous shade of purple. It was no great revelation that Toothman survived in his job by pilfering, parroting, and relying upon the insights of others.

"Of course I will take a look," he stated nonchalantly before turning to exit. As I followed the others from the small dining room, my eyes settled fleetingly on the crippled timepiece lying at my feet. What a shame, I thought, that the elegant antique would be removed from service as a result of a careless impulse.

Sunlight was shimmering across the surface of glass-skinned towers as trading opened the next day with a fresh round of hand-to-hand combat between the buyers and sellers of stock. I didn't need to be there to know that the typical scene was unfolding on the institutional stock desk at Platt Brothers. Traders were shouting and waving their arms. Salesmen were mumbling into telephone receivers. And a dim electronic hum on the open floor accompanied blinking lights and flashing computer monitors. Tom McGuire picked up my call on the first ring.

"Hey, Mac, it's Nate Perkins—and *please* do not make a spectacle of the fact I am on the phone." I could tell that my admonition had taken all the fun out of this phone call to my pot-bellied ex-colleague.

"Listen, I'd like you to do me a favor, and I'm hoping you can keep it pretty discreet, okay?"

"Sure, buddy," responded McGuire with a chortle. "It's not often I get to speak directly with the really smart money." McGuire was relishing the chance to tweak me without sounding insincere.

"We're thinking of putting a major short on in the airlines,"
I said, lowering my voice to almost a whisper. "But I want to
get a good gauge on the sentiment on these stocks before we
dive in. The prices have already started rolling over, and I want
to ensure that all the bad news isn't already priced into the
stocks."

I concluded with my request. "Can you call Toothman and
press him for some updated feedback on how he's feeling about
the group? I don't mind if you tell him that you are responding
to a customer inquiry, but I ask for your word that you do not
tell him that the inquiry came from me."

"No problem at all, old buddy. I'm on it."

My unexpected call had given the aimless McGuire a
roadmap for getting through what otherwise promised to be
a long day. I had no doubt that his first calls would go out
to a number of his top clients, and that he would confide in
secret mumbles that the airlines were about to get torpedoed
by smart-money short sellers. And as those clients stepped into
the market to clip the stocks, they would bump into supply
that was already battering the shares as the fund managers who
worked at the companies represented by the junior researchers
at Toothman's dinner also liquidated positions. After a suitable
intermission to allow his clients a chance to get trades completed,
McGuire would call Kent Toothman. Feigning alarm and
dripping with compliments, the veteran stock hustler would
insist that the client base was clamoring for Toothman to lend
some authoritative research insight to the state of the airline
industry and the outlook for the stocks.

I later learned that, shortly after midday, Kent Toothman bounded onto the trading floor at Platt Brothers and picked up an ordinary looking white phone. The hoot-and-holler was an intercom system that sat on the desk of every salesman and every trader in every Platt office all over the world. It was reserved for use in special circumstances, to announce breaking news, critical firm-wide announcements, and for "break-in" research calls that were considered too urgent and time-sensitive to wait for unveiling in the morning meeting. Kent Toothman considered that he was making just such a big call.

"This is Kent Toothman. We are downgrading all of the airline stocks to sell!" he shouted into the telephone receiver. "Earnings estimates are being slashed for all of the companies. National Airways numbers are coming down the hardest—details in the morning meeting tomorrow..."

And with that message delivered, he would raise his chin high, with a smug air of triumph. Brokers loved break-in calls because it gave them a new jolt of adrenaline when the day began to drag, after they had picked off every digestible morsel from the morning call. They rarely had reason to call their clients twice in the same day.

Instantly news wires were reporting Platt's downgrade of the airlines as Toothman made a small victory lap around the trading floor before retreating back down to his office, where he would find his first batch of phone messages in several weeks. Across town, I stared into my computer monitor as the spirits of bedlam broke loose. Every airline stock, which had been already falling in the morning trading, gapped down another five percent on the news of the Platt Brothers downgrade. National Airlines, which had traded four times its normal daily trading volume in the session through noon, was halted for trading by the New York Stock Exchange as the result of an order imbalance, meaning that the volume of incoming sell orders had overwhelmed offsetting buy orders on the books. Twenty minutes later, the NYSE changed the reason for the halt to "news pending."

The burly receptionist at Tantalus, whom I had subsequently learned was named Patrick, knocked at my glass-walled window, and I waved for him to enter. He dropped a third message on my desk, indicating that Tom McGuire had called yet again to speak with me. The box marked "important" was checked. I nodded curtly at the piece of paper, crumpled it up, and dispatched it to my trashcan, where it would join its two older siblings. I returned my attention to the computer monitor and noticed instantly that National Airways had just issued a press release. I could feel profits gushing into Tantalus as I slowly digested the words.

Due to unusual trading activity in its shares, National Airways Corporation has decided to issue a preliminary estimate of its earnings expectations for the upcoming fourth fiscal quarter. The company currently anticipates a loss of between $1.25 and $1.75 per share due to the extraordinary recent pressure on the company's costs and revenues. The company will make no further public communication until it reports its final results.

My room was spinning and my vision blurred. I thought briefly of Vinod Sharma. Squinting to refocus my eyes, I checked my computer screen again to see that National Airways shares were indicated for trading down another ten dollars from the last price before they had been halted. Patrick banged again on my office door and delivered a new message from Tom McGuire.

"Have very large seller of National Airways," it read. The word *very* was written in all capital letters. Lucas Orr appeared in my doorway.

"Well done," he said. "Stop by my office after the closing bell." His face seemed strangely angular as he turned and walked away. I spent the next thirty minutes in sullen reflection, trying to fathom whether a mind, once twisted with the intensity of a new concept, could ever regain its original contours.

∽

Lucas Orr looked up from his desk, and his face brightened when I trudged slowly into his office shortly after the four o'clock market close.

"Ah, Nate. From your dashed demeanor I can tell that you are feeling a sensation something like regret, perhaps even self-loathing." The master's ability to interpret body language was as keen as his ability to sniff out meaning in the financial markets.

"Well," I said slowly, revealing my distress by a lame attempt at sarcasm, "the part of me that enjoys draining the blood, drop by drop, from a person's career—like we did to that chap Sharma—is feeling great pleasure. I only regret that I was unable to inflict physical pain on our subject as well." As soon as I spoke, I knew that my outburst would serve no purpose.

Orr took an extra second or two to look me over before using my discomfort as a teaching moment.

"Three lessons you must embrace, Nate. First, never reveal your emotions. Never. Your foe must not know whether it is rage or remorse welling up inside of you. When you open a view through the window into your feelings, you have lost," he said bluntly.

"Second, you need to focus less on the act and more on its intent. In this instance, we merely plucked out some unsightly ragweed before it could take over the garden. If it had not been us, and if it had not been now, make no mistake—it would have happened soon. Highstone was on a collision course with disaster."

"Go on," I said, curious to learn how Orr would justify his actions.

"Highstone was desperate to maintain its early performance results, but they had had a series of disappointing quarters. Investors were threatening to pull out their assets, and the firm had been leveraging their investment portfolio with borrowed money to improve their numbers. As their panic grew, they were taking larger and more speculative bets. The trouble and ultimate loss would only have been larger if these malignant roots had been allowed to undermine the healthy vegetation."

Orr had just described our devastation of another firm as a public service, akin to weeding a garden. It was a cunning way to think about our system of making money, but I couldn't help feeling it was somewhat specious.

"And the third?" I asked.

"Be more parsimonious about where you apportion your sympathy. This benighted magician Munson Erlich, a man with three homes and a yacht, recently fired a chauffeur who had been working for him for ten years when the man had the audacity to ask for time off to care for a pregnant wife and a sick child. An ass is but an ass, though laden with gold."

Once again, Lucas Orr stood tall, a man in a white hat. Then he suddenly steered the conversation in a new direction.

"Here is what I wanted to tell you," he continued matter-of-factly. "Newman has resigned from the firm." I felt a momentary sensation of gasping for breath. I was working in a deep subterranean cavern, and my torch had just flickered and gone out. Newman was my translator when it came to the arcane methods of Tantalus, and he was also the only friend I had made at the firm. I thought we had begun to understand each other.

"Why?" I asked as coolly as I could.

"There comes a time for all things." I felt that Orr's chill gaze was penetrating my soul as his face was again bathed in the dusky space of the dimly lit office. "Newman had played out his possibilities here with us and needed—*personally*—to move on."

We both sat quietly as I experienced an oppressive feeling of loneliness. A stray beam of fading western sunshine that had been peeking under the bottom of a slightly elevated window blind slowly disappeared from my field of vision. For a moment I wanted to chase that hopeful ray of light and burst through the walls that felt as though they were closing in on me.

Orr spoke again. "This will mean great things for you Nate—for us. I will need to rely on you, increasingly. You should be pleased."

I sat unmoving and still silent. Orr broke the impasse.

"Come," he commanded. "We will talk—really talk."

Orr pressed a few buttons on his telephone and spoke into the receiver so quietly that I couldn't hear what he was saying. Then he bounded out from behind his desk and grabbed his gray fedora, tugging briefly on my sleeve without actually touching me, and he motioned toward the door. We quickly moved past the office of the enigmatic Malpas, who looked up to smile at me for the first time. Then he quickly resumed his bent posture over a stack of papers. Next door, Newman's office was dark and empty, confirming my fear that I had probably seen him for the last time. A few more steps and I turned into my own space, raising my arm to indicate to Orr that I needed a moment before continuing on.

When I went into my office, I immediately noticed something unexpected. A square, yellow Post-it note was affixed to my telephone receiver. Newman had scrawled a message in his barely legible handwriting. It simply said, "Good luck. Ted." I suspected that this would serve as the final word from my friend.

Moments later I was joining Orr in the dark sedan with tinted windows, which I had often seen idling near the curbside of our building. It rode low on its tires, an indication that it was heavily armored. The world of money had reached a point when many of the chief executives of Wall Street firms found it necessary to travel like heads of state, in cars with bulletproof glass, special tires, and armored bodies. Patrick turned from the driver's seat and gave me a grin. Then he pulled directly into the rush of oncoming traffic. Several yellow cabs veered to avoid our vehicle as Patrick navigated onto the elevated Park Avenue causeway, where north- and southbound lanes split to flank Grand Central Station. The roadway then passed alongside a looming, homely building soaring into the skies above us. The sixty-story office tower, once known as the Pan Am Building, had been the world's largest commercial building when it was built in the 1960s. In financial circles, it was infamous because a legendary 1970s financier had used his briefcase to shatter a window so he could leap to his death. Several years later Pan Am sold the building, and its prominent logo was pulled down from the north and south façades. We sped through a short tunnel before the split roadways converged again, spilling back onto the grand concourse of Park Avenue.

Patrick navigated uptown for several minutes before turning west and wrapping around to Fifth Avenue. The car was met at curbside by a doorman who pulled Orr's door open without speaking. I glanced briefly up and down the alpha road of Manhattan, bordered on its western edge by the browning foliage of Central Park and on the eastern edge by a canyon of buildings that housed the city's most financially fortunate citizens. Several strides later I followed Orr into the lobby of a building that I had previously thought was merely a grand hotel. It was, but it also had a special entrance to apartments for those who wished the ultimate in service and could pay enormous prices to live in a kind of hybrid magnificence. We entered an elevator and rode in silence to the highest floors.

Over the next several hours, Orr took me on a tour of his private empyrean. The apartment occupied the three penthouse floors of the building, connected by an internal staircase with a sweeping mahogany banister. Arched windows twice the size of a standing man framed a massive ballroom that occupied an entire floor. The lustrous dark tones of finely crafted floorboards and polished black tile contrasted with the simplicity of creamy linen wallpaper and white ceilings. The blizzard of white was regularly interrupted by the flash of gold—massive gilded frames of Old Masters oil paintings, shimmering branches of chandeliers, and the subtle alloy of exquisitely detailed wall sconces and table clocks. An almost youthful breezy tone enlivened Orr's voice as he explained the intricate details of the three-year project that had restored his residence. It had taken another two years to appoint it with the finest artwork from galleries in New York and London. The room, indeed the entire apartment, had the aura of a European museum. The impression of a public space was underscored by the fact that there was not a single personal photograph on display, even in the smaller, private rooms. The absence of the images of Orr's family and friends created the sense that the place could be turned over to someone else with the same lavish tastes, and there would be no sense of who had lived here before.

Orr had uncorked a bottle of wine when we began our tour, and he replenished my glass as we passed a life-sized kneeling Egyptian figure that he identified as fourth century. We toasted each other several times as the sensation of finely aged grape began to take hold. When our second bottle of midcentury Mouton-Rothschild, with its simple label of red and black arrows, had run dry, Orr delicately uncorked a specimen that he cradled and caressed with such pride and affection that I wondered whether he had his own vineyard somewhere in France. The complex traces of oak and leather and licorice swirled together and lingered on my senses as we imbibed a wine of such quality that even I, who was hardly an expert, knew that I was drinking something magnificent and rare.

It was around seven thirty when we heard a chime, and Orr led me to the dining room. We sat facing each other across a long table that could seat twenty comfortably. I paused instinctively to speak a blessing to myself and became aware that Orr was eying me closely. Aborting my prayer in mid-thought, I quickly tucked into a savory, aromatic plate of tender pheasant breast and infant vegetables, which been set neatly at our places before we sat down. Orr ate very little. When dinner was finished, he refilled our goblets, and we moved on into the next room.

I was none too steady on my feet by then, and I collapsed into the firm embrace of a deep, leather sofa. I watched while Orr pressed a recessed wood panel and a hinged door opened to reveal a stacked panel of knobs, switches, and small green and red lights. He twiddled with the equipment, and the room soon softened to a hazy amber glow while smoky chords of jazz wafted quietly from hidden speakers. Orr sat in a chair opposite me and began one of his scholarly discourses, this one on the meaning of African masks, of which he had an ominous collection arrayed in the foyer, just visible over his shoulder. His hands flew in animation—as though the spirits had inspired him—as he revealed the mysteries of these vessels of the supernatural world. I thought that I had judged him unfairly. Here, in the comfort of his home, removed from the savagery of his cutthroat profession, Lucas Orr was just a very rich human being with a passion for art and the ability to satisfy it. My growing admiration for him reinforced my tingling sensation of contentment.

Orr was telling me the story of one of his artifacts, a mask that had been worn for ceremonies to assure fertility and abundance, when I interjected. "Is this what you always wanted? I mean, when you were growing up—when you dreamed—could you ever have imagined you would achieve all of this?" I made a sweep of my arms across the expanse of his perfectly opulent den.

Orr sipped from his goblet. He smiled quickly, and his lean frame reclined as he reflected. He slipped off his soft black kidskin shoes and stretched his legs on top of the inlaid mahogany coffee table in front of him. He nodded slowly several times and looked at me curiously, as though considering whether to answer my question.

"Nate, what does it matter? If I was educated at Oxford, or even if I am the orphaned son of an impoverished family from the Midwest, would that change who I am?"

"Uh, well..."

"The way I see it, there are two kinds of people, and they try to arrange their lives differently. Some have a fixed, immovable plan. Every action is designed to move them closer to their goals. And then there are those who react to circumstances as they unfold, making decisions based on vagaries and fate." The hazy lighting made his eyes seem dark and unreadable. I cleared my throat but did not speak.

"You can judge whether I am the former or the latter. Just know one thing—nothing material in the ample collections that surround us defines me." And then he rose and strode from the room.

I sat alone, oblivious to the subtle creep of time, lulled by the entrancing potion of wine and music. A melody of bells chimed from an antique English clock across the luxurious expanse. At some point I heard footsteps. Orr, I thought. But when I opened my eyes, I saw and smelled a fragrant feminine creature in a silk caftan who floated across the floor and gracefully arranged herself next to me on the sofa.

"Jasmin," she said extending a hand that was firm but soft. I recognized her as the beautiful woman with the large, brown eyes whom I had seen inside Orr's dark sedan.

"Are you disappointed to see me instead of Luc?" Her accent was slightly foreign, and her face was uncomfortably close to mine. I was looking into the eyes of a siren who seemed to have been conjured up from the *Arabian Nights*. I pulled back and peered helplessly around the room to see if Orr was coming back, but we were alone. Jasmin reached across me to refill my wine glass, and as she did, she let her body drape itself across me.

"Drink," she said softly, raising the glass to my lips, and I did. Then she moved the crystal to her own mouth, letting the perfect taste linger softly on her tongue. She never took her eyes from mine, and I could feel her exerting her power over me. I finally managed to muster up some meaningless sounds from the trembling void within me.

"Umm…are you a friend of Mr. Orr's? I mean…do you live here? No, I mean…" Jasmin smiled, and tiny creases formed at the corner of her mouth. I had thought she was about my age, but as I looked at her, I realized she was older and certainly more sophisticated than I.

"Luc and I were lovers once, and sometimes we are lovers still, but above all, we are friends. He is my protector, and I am—well, I am here when he wants me. We are close, but even so, I can't say that I really know him. Perhaps you will come to take Luc as I do. He is what he does, he says what he means, and he has no past. For him, only the present and the future exist," she said, as though that was enough for anyone to know. I opened my mouth to say something although I wasn't sure what, but Jasmin moved her fingers and touched my lips to stop me.

"*Shhhh...* we should not be talking about Luc. This is your night." She caressed my mouth and stroked the outline of my chin, which had sprouted a dense growth of stubble since I shaved that morning, so many hours ago. Then she took my hand and led me away, past the wooden eyes of the spirit world and down a hall. In a room with a vaulted ceiling, her warm body slithered across mine, offering pleasure and asking for nothing in return. My resistance was broken with the intensity of a violent storm, and I succumbed.

I awoke to a splitting headache and faint streaks of cobalt breaking through the darkness of a muted city. I was alone in the bedroom where my evening had ended. Quickly gathering up my clothes and dressing, I decided to leave as quietly as I could. As I entered the foyer, I felt a chill breeze. Orr was already awake. The french doors to the terrace were open, and he stood outside, wrapped in a woolen dressing gown, gazing over a waking metropolis. It was the first time I had seen him hatless while out of doors. He gestured, and I joined him.

"Do you know why they build magnificent structures like these, Nate?" he asked.

I stood at his side and waited for him to answer his own question. The broad expanse of Central Park drifted below us in the softening dawn. Beyond the park we could begin to see the faint outlines of the buildings on Central Park West as Manhattan was rising from her slumber. A red light flickered, barely visible in the distance.

"In every civilization, some of us are chosen to rise above the suffering, the filth, the struggle for everyday survival. Can you imagine a world in which the innovators, the thinkers, the creators cannot insulate themselves from the moribund, the ashes, the cruelty, and the decay?" Orr asked. The treetops and ponds and small buildings of the park were slowly emerging from beneath the murkiness.

"Us?" I thought out loud.

"What kind of world would it be without the industrial genius of George Eastman or the literary brilliance of Hemingway? Where would we be without the towers of Fifth Avenue?" he continued. Light was overtaking the cityscape as it unfolded in front of us, and I knew that my time with him was fleeting.

"Uh...about last night." I shifted uncomfortably. "I just want you to know that there is a woman...I care for her very much."

Orr was silent, focused on the red light across the park.

"This woman, her name is Dana...she was the one who helped us with the Simpson Chemical investment." I said, oozing vulnerability.

"Lucas, she believes in me...I hope you understand."

Orr turned to face me for the first time since I had walked onto the terrace. He smiled benevolently and unconsciously touched the cowlick that stuck up on top of his head. Then he patted my shoulder and turned to walk inside, but he stopped as we heard a dog barking sharply on the street below.

"Dogs," Luc said, and he paused. "They are the most dangerous of all creatures." I looked at him questioningly.

"Yes," he said. "Dangerous. If you have a dog, it is almost inevitable that, unless you are a monster, you will come to love it. Few things in this world are certain, but you can be almost sure that, because a dog's life is so much shorter than a human's, it will die before you do, and you will mourn." He paused a moment before continuing.

"A piece of advice," he said. "You may think you love this girl, Dana, and she may love you or hurt you. But if you lose her, you will not grieve for her the way you would grieve for a faithful dog who will never betray you. Long after you no longer dream about Dana, you will wake up one night crying because, for a moment, you felt as though your dog was nuzzled up against your back in bed."

This was such an unexpected outpouring that there was little I could think of to say. I nodded, attempting to look wise, and thanked Luc for an unforgettable evening. Returning home to change into fresh clothes, I picked up coffee and a muffin and arrived at the office at my usual time. I realized that in five days it would be Christmas.

CHAPTER SEVEN

When Commodore Vanderbilt's favored youngest son, George Washington Vanderbilt, died, the Commodore, already a choleric man, became further hardened. Young George, named after his father's boyhood idol, had represented something significant in the mind of the father. George had attended West Point and had plunged eagerly into his nation's service as an infantry captain when the Civil War broke out. At Shiloh, George had contracted tuberculosis. After spending nearly two years wasting away in a series of nursing hospitals, the smartest and most promising of Vanderbilt's offspring died at the unripe age of twenty-five. The young man was buried in a quiet ceremony near Vanderbilt's parents in a private area of the Moravian Cemetery on Staten Island that was reserved exclusively for the use of the family. Fighting his private sorrow, the Commodore plunged into the most productive phase of his life's work in business.

In the financial world, the holiday weeks that bracketed Christmas were either a time of cheer or of despair. This was when the counting of bounty superseded the counting of blessings. As profits were tabulated and bonuses distributed, careers were made and lost.

With the dial turned toward a new year, I could feel the invisible tug of the puppeteer as Tantalus worked overtime to find our next big conquest. But my labors became lonelier and less satisfying. I missed the companionship of Newman. I tried several times to track him down, even contacting the alumni offices at Harvard and Yale, but the searches came up empty. Newman had vanished, and it seemed that he was not interested in being found.

As winter receded into spring, Wall Street began to heat up again. Stock prices had staged a modest but steady recovery from the crash, and as it became clear that the economy would avoid a protracted downturn, the stock promoters clambered out of hibernation. That was good news for Tantalus because the two-headed beast of euphoria and speculation was the animal we hunted.

Occasionally, McGuire would call to regale me with gossip or recount some preposterous burlesque that he had perpetrated on an unwitting colleague. Frolic and farce was a form of aspiration for my ex-colleague; without the fresh air of new tricks, he might asphyxiate.

"Perk, I know you are a big-shot hedge fund guy now, but you gotta' hear this one," he blustered over the telephone one afternoon.

"All ears for you, Mac."

"Well you know how the lotto is up to like a hundred million bucks?" he asked.

"Um, yeah," I said, although I had never bought a lotto ticket; trading on Wall Street was enough of a lottery for me.

"Turns out that our pious little friend Henry Fitton is something of a lottery addict. I discovered about fifty tickets in his drawer for the big drawing." As with most of McGuire's capers, I had no idea where he was going with the story.

"The minute the winning numbers get announced, I go out and purchase the exact same numbers, but for the next available drawing. Then I go to the office after hours and tuck the new ticket—with winning numbers, but the wrong date—deep into the stash in Fitton's drawer."

"Uh-oh," I said. I could see where the escapade was headed.

"So Fitton arrives at the office early the next morning, and I watch him sideways as he carefully sifts through his stack of tickets. By the time he finds the one I had bought for him, he is obviously only scanning the numbers, not looking at the dates. Why would he? He bought the tickets himself—he thinks."

"Oh, no."

"Oh, yeah," shouted McGuire. "Suddenly, he looks like he is jolted with a current of electricity. He spends several minutes shaking as though he's in a revival meeting trance and then jumps to his feet and unleashes a torrent of obscenities like you have never heard. The gist of it that he despises us all and he hates the business and that we have seen the last of Henry Fitton. And then he rushes out of the office!"

"Did he return to the hateful job?" I asked, wondering how much damage McGuire's trick might have done to Fitton's chances of getting his desk back.

"Yeah. Later that very afternoon," McGuire said and chuckled. "Never even raised his head from the phone for two straight hours."

໐ᴗ໐

The distractions from across the river soon became a sideshow, despite my conviction that Dana and I were meant to be together. As the weeks passed, I began to feel a certain kind of energy around the Tantalus offices, as if there was a new idea gestating. When I went to see Orr to insinuate my way onto the new project, he greeted me with an uncharacteristic coolness. It was clear that, at least for the moment, he was keeping me in the dark on a looming investment scheme.

For several days I stewed in isolation, sitting in my office until well after dark. A riddle of my own creation began to gnaw at me during these idle hours of reflection. I played the last twelve months of my life backward and forward in my mind, pausing to reflect on the meanings of words and the significance of chance events. When I could no longer abide this curious hunger, I delivered a message to Malpas, who seemingly functioned as the firm's chief operating officer as well as its chief legal counsel—although like everyone else in the eccentric place, he didn't have a job title.

"I need to take several days out of the office," I said. My tone was a little crisper than it probably should have been. I handed him a short, handwritten note declaring my intent. As I was leaving his office, I was surprised to hear Malpas calling me back.

"Perkins, there is actually a matter of some sensitivity that I need to discuss with you. Please close the door and sit down." The gravelly voice was distinctly not amiable. I did as I was told.

"Yes?" I looked Malpas in the eye, but I was uneasy. Lucas Orr was a mystery, but he permitted glimpses into his private world. Malpas was entirely opaque. The only reason I knew anything about him at all was that one day after work, when I was on my way to a movie theatre in the East Sixties, I walked through a side street of townhouses and saw the door opened by a butler. As Malpas exited, I heard the butler wish him a "pleasant evening, sir." His car was waiting at the curb, and he slid into the backseat alone and drove off. Those who live in townhouses in New York, rather than in cooperatives, often do so because they are not willing to undergo the scrutiny of a co-op's board of directors and the requirement to submit complete financial statements and undergo an interview. I was pretty certain that Malpas would consider such a process to be akin to dancing naked in the street. Or walking—I couldn't imagine him dancing anywhere, with or without clothing.

Malpas announced, "It has come to my attention that you seemingly misappropriated a proprietary piece of information in the possession of this firm while you were still employed at

Platt Brothers, and you traded on this inside information for your personal financial gain." The steely gaze of my accuser penetrated me like a sharpened rapier.

"I did what?" Then I suddenly felt sick to my stomach, recognizing that Malpas was referring to my well-timed—and meagerly profitable—purchase of Bonham Corporation shares, a transaction I barely remembered.

"But...you...I...Newman mentioned the idea to me. It was information that I received from Tantalus," I said. I was stammering and could hear that I sounded pathetic.

"To be clear, Perkins, this was information that our firm never acted upon. And the reason that we did not do so is because it represented material nonpublic information that had come into our possession by happenstance. The rules about trading on inside information are extremely clear. And the penalties are similarly unambiguous." Malpas had me dangling helplessly, on a precarious ledge. But just as quickly he offered a hand.

"We are working with our lawyers on this—perhaps there is some area of gray that could explain this blatant transgression. You just stay cool, Perkins, and I will see what I can do." Debilitated and defenseless, I nodded.

"Okay. I understand."

"Just remember, Perkins, you're not in Kansas anymore," Malpas lampooned me with a grin. I quickly retreated from the office, stunned to learn that Newman had played a role in this orchestrated treachery. I needed to find some fresh air.

The crush of traffic and pedestrians seemed to press closer with each step I took, and I realized that the streets of New York at midday were not likely to provide the place for reflection that I so desperately needed. My hands dug deep into my coat pockets as I stretched my arms, backing up against the side of a building to survey the frenetic scene around me. When the fingers of my right hand retrieved a business card from my pocket, an item that I had long since forgotten, I had found my destination.

"Ah, Mr. Perkins, the financial sleuth. I was hoping that you would take me up on my offer to have you stop by." Duncan Bridges seemed truly delighted to see me, his head wobbling loosely, just as I remembered. Bridges Capital occupied a portion of the eighth floor in a nondescript steel and glass building in the middle of one of the darker midtown cross-streets.

"Rosa, can you get our guest a drink—and perhaps something to eat. A sandwich maybe?" Bridges and his receptionist were both eying me curiously.

"Just water would be fine." I followed Bridges through a small warren of cubicles, where the chatter of friendly conversation wafted up through the open work spaces. A short, carpeted hallway led to his office. The walls were hung on both sides with black-and-white photographs of New York, and the carpet showed the wear of age, with a few coffee spots massaged into the fabric. Bridges' office looked down onto the street below, and the windows had no blinds. It was clear that the sunshine had a hard time finding its way to the lower floors of a midblock building in the caverns of midtown. He plopped himself into a creaky wooden chair and peered out between towers of paper that framed his cluttered desk as I sat opposite him.

"You work for a high-stress employer, eh?" The soft pouches under his eyes gave Bridges a kindly look.

"Do you know Lucas Orr?" I asked, suddenly panicked about why I had come.

"Relax, I don't work for Lucas Orr. He has no power here." Bridges stood and walked to the window.

"Kent Toothman told me that you were once a salesman at Platt Brothers. That is, before you came over to the buy side." Hearing that Bridges had done some poking around about my background would have ordinarily made me suspicious, but something about the dog-eared ordinariness of his office set me at ease. I wanted to trust him.

"Yeah, I sort of stumbled into this job; lucky, I guess." The way I said that made the good luck part of it sound doubtful.

"Did you know that I worked at Platt Brothers once, way back in the Dark Ages? I was actually one of the first analysts they hired when they started the research department."

"Really?" I was genuinely intrigued by our shared heritage. "What sector did you cover?"

"That was actually part of the problem. I didn't have direct responsibility for any single industry. I picked up stocks— typically the firm's banking clients—when they fell through the cracks or when no one else wanted to cover them. They called me a 'special situations' analyst. So when I put a sell rating on one of the firm's best corporate clients, it was pretty much all downhill from there. In any case, I really wanted to hang out my own shingle, control my own destiny—you know. And though I still have some good friends at the firm, I have never regretted leaving."

I was staring at the series of stock charts strewn all over Bridges' desk. "You are probably wondering why I am spending time looking at graphs, right?" I nodded.

"The inputs of my investment process only involve two variables: price and volume. This may sound a little strange to you, trafficking as you do in numbers and stories and spreadsheets and hidden innuendo, but my world is simpler than that." Bridges was punching some keystrokes into his desktop computer.

"A company's stock price incorporates all available information, both the publicly disclosed variety and the inside tidbits obscured from public view. Simply put, everyone who buys or sells a stock is acting on the best possible information they have available. That goes for the small retail investor in Des Moines reacting to a neighbor's gossip, or the savvy mind inside a towering New York hedge fund who has obtained the choicest morsel of insight." Duncan Bridges' investment approach was a relief in its simplicity.

"And, naturally, the more confident the point of view, the larger the investment commitment. All of this information, some trivial and some precious, is crystallized in the price of the stock and the volume of shares traded. So—see—come over here." He was motioning for me to walk around the back of his desk, where he was studying a stock price chart with lines and bars in several colors on his monitor.

"This is what I call a happy stock. The price has drifted down over a period of time and then traded sideways on low volume, reflecting investor apathy. And then, here," he was pointing to an inflection in the chart, "it begins to turn upwards on increasing volume. This beginning of the uptrend line completes the smile. Somebody knows something, and they are committing large dollars to their bullish view at a time when the sellers have been exhausted. I don't even need to know what information is motivating that buyer—I just know that I need to become a buyer at that point as well."

"And I suppose that a sad stock would be one with the inverse characteristics?" I asked, tracing the trajectory of an inverted smile in the air.

"You are a quick study, Nate—can I call you Nate? I could use someone like you around here."

The bluntness of his proposal startled me. I wondered whether Bridges thought he was poaching me or rescuing me. I glanced briefly around his office, which wasn't much better decorated than a college dorm common room. A squash racquet and what appeared to be a gym bag had been casually tossed on a plaid sofa, the only other furniture in the office. I struggled for the right words.

"I really appreciate that. I mean—you never know. But, right now, I can't really turn my back on Tantalus. They have given me a great opportunity." I paused. Bridges did not speak as he sensed I wanted to continue.

"I do have some things I need to sort out in my mind. Do you know anything about my firm?"

"I certainly know the firm by reputation. My opinion? You are swimming in the shark tank." Duncan Bridges was leaning back in thought, both hands locked behind his head.

"Well, is the shark tank safe?" I asked.

"That depends on whether you are a shark or a sea lion." The riddle wasn't helping me to resolve my dilemma, so I decided to trust him and chose the direct approach.

"I don't know," I said. "I certainly don't want to be prey, but I don't really feel like a natural predator either. Luc Orr has convinced me that when we take down a weak company, we're doing a cleanup job for the market. Sometimes I think he's right, but other times, I think it's just an excuse for vulture capitalism. The fact is, I can't make sense of my boss or the company I'm working for. What would you do if you were in my shoes?"

"Have you ever talked to Leonard Colesmith?" Bridges was holding his chin in his hand, studying me intently to see whether that name meant anything to me.

"Colesmith...oh yes, Colesmith—the one who originally hired Lucas Orr. Maybe I should talk to him—start in the beginning. To be honest, I'm not sure exactly what I want to know; there's nothing specific. I mean, nothing illegal. But something keeps gnawing at me. If you don't mind my borrowing your ocean analogy, sometimes I feel like a fish out of water. Do you think Colesmith would talk to me?"

"He might, but I only met him a couple of times, very casually, a long time ago. I don't think he and Orr ended on good terms, and after their partnership was over, he disappeared. I haven't even heard his name for years."

"Do you have any idea where I could find him?"

"Unfortunately, I don't. But perhaps you should try. You probably won't find contentment until you have some answers."

Sensing that there was nothing more to say, I stood up. Duncan Bridges extended his hand. "I am glad you came to see me. Please don't hesitate to stop by again."

೧൭

The main branch of the New York Public Library is built atop a two-block section of Fifth Avenue that once served as home to the Croton Reservoir, which supplied drinking water to a thirsty, booming city in the nineteenth century. The entrance to the imposing marble structure is guarded by two stone lions, famously nicknamed "Patience" and "Fortitude" by Mayor La Guardia because he felt that Gotham's citizens would need those qualities to survive the Great Depression. Fortitude is located on the north, and Patience is on the south. Inside, in the main entry hall, an inscription in gold lettering declares that the building is to be maintained forever. Twin marble staircases, smooth and curved by the footsteps of scholars and dreamers, led to my destination, the building's third-floor public reading room.

Duncan Bridges had forged a new mission for me as I entered this chandeliered chapel of knowledge. Ceiling murals dappled with blue sky and lavender clouds soared above me. Massive windows streamed winter sunshine into the cavernous room neatly lined with wood tables and ringed by tall bookshelves. I soon discovered that the thousands of volumes visible in the main reading room were primarily for show. Most of the library's millions of books and documents were archived out of view, to be retrieved from subterranean storerooms. I made a few hasty notations on a call slip and handed my request into the bony grip of a pale-eyed librarian.

It didn't take long before she returned with a simple white box labeled "Manhattan White Pages, 1976." I retreated to an anteroom that housed a microfilm machine, and scanning through the pages of film, I found what I was looking for.

The blurry entry projected on the screen in front of me gave evidence to that fact that there was a time not long past when successful businessmen did not believe a phone book listing lowered or endangered them. The entry I was seeking read, "*Colesmith, Leonard.*" I copied the address and returned the borrowed data spool to the call desk.

I took a taxi uptown, arriving in front of the green awning leading into a well-appointed building in the East Seventies. The heavy doors into a dimly lit lobby were opened by a thickset doorman, whose obvious intent was to block my way until he discovered whom I was visiting. He wasn't young, and his stoop and heavy tread suggested that he had worked at the building long enough to be able to answer my question.

"Colesmith," I said firmly. "I am here to see Mr. Colesmith." He squinted suspiciously and stepped closer.

"Mr. Colesmith has not lived here for many, many years."

My next statement would determine the success or failure of my quest. I immediately thrust my hand into the fleshy, unsuspecting grasp of the doorman.

"My name is Nathaniel Perkins, and I really, really need your assistance," I said, looking at him innocently and eagerly. It was one of the times when the Midwestern manners I'd learned long ago came to my assistance.

"I am working for Mr. Colesmith's old firm, and we recently reopened a case that is over ten years old. We are coming up empty on some of the key facts, and Mr. Colesmith is the missing link. I desperately need to find him to ask some questions. I need his help."

I hunched forward submissively, a petitioner. The doorman blinked, deliberating, and turned away, opening the door into a side room. He returned with a scrap of paper, on which he had scrawled a phone number in halting, uneven handwriting.

"This is all I have. Tell Mr. Colesmith that Wolf sends his best," he said in a tone that suggested nostalgia. I nodded appreciatively and hurried back into the street.

Within minutes I was nervously dialing the seven digits, looking for the man who might be able to help mollify my lingering suspicions.

"Mr. Colesmith, my name is Nathaniel Perkins. I—um—I am calling from the office of Lucas Orr." My introduction was met with complete silence.

"I, uh, the reason I am calling is that I was wondering if I could talk to you about Mr. Orr, ask you a few questions."

"*No!*" The silence was crushed by a sudden eruption of sheer anger. "I am not sure who you are or what you really want, but the answer is no. Not now, not ever. And do not call back—because I will not answer!"

Colesmith's outraged response to my unexpected call was not altogether surprising. My early training at Tantalus had trained me for these sorts of obstacles. I quickly confirmed that

Colesmith's phone number was unlisted, preventing me from quickly discovering his address. How ironic, I thought, that at the height of his professional career in New York his address was publicly listed, but in anonymous retirement he had purged his entry from the phone books. Soon I was back at the New York Public Library, plunging into a deep study that would allow me to crack the cipher represented by Colesmith's phone number. The area code by itself would only tell me what state he lived in, but it was a big state, and I was in a hurry.

Within an hour, I had learned some interesting facts about the history of the development of telephone exchanges. The original Bell interests had planned to exploit their patent commercially by the manufacture and sale of a telephone apparatus. The plan was that the purchasers of this equipment would contract with outside suppliers for point-to-point connection services. But the Bell Company soon recognized that the future belonged to the service providers, and they set about creating central office switchboards, where in the early days, subscribers were connected through operators by simply using personal names as identifiers. A measles epidemic in Lowell, Massachusetts, soon revealed the vulnerabilities of such a design, with any panic able to quickly overwhelm the finite number of working line punchers.

The next advancement in the development of the phone networks was represented by the creation of fixed local exchanges, often characterized by the first two numbers of the phone number taking on letter identifiers. So a request for "UNderwood-4668," would represent a call to the phone number 86-4668, in a continuous geographical region that served all phone numbers commencing with the digits 86. Over time, letter identifiers fell away, and as the demand for phone numbers exploded, two-digit exchanges became three-digit prefixes, and eventually area codes further expanded the possibilities of a complex digital network. But after a hundred years of evolution, I discovered that the three-digit prefix within a given area code still identified a specific place. Digging through a series of phone books, I had soon narrowed the Colesmith phone number down to a handful of towns on Cape Cod. I was intrigued with the discovery that Lucas Orr's mentor hadn't settled in the Hamptons, like so many wrinkled Wall Street financiers. With an additional analysis of real estate records and local attractions, I had further refined my search to two affluent beach towns on the Cape.

Once I decided what to do, it occurred to me that I might be able to convince Dana to join me for a weekend of fun and mystery solving. I had not seen much of her since the Sunday we had lunched with her family. I had also become aware in brief, flavorless phone calls that she had "crossed the wall" and was working on a very big and time-consuming deal for Platt Brothers, an assignment that frequently took her out of town.

The "Chinese wall" referred to the legal separation that existed between investment bankers and research analysts at Wall Street firms. The investment bankers served corporate clients and were in frequent contact with privileged "inside" information about pending acquisitions, stock offerings, and other sensitive stock-moving data. The research analysts, by contrast, served public investors, and to retain their credibility—as well as their honesty—they were restricted from coming into contact with information that existed on the other side of the Chinese wall. On rare occasions, however, a firm would consider the input of a research analyst so vital to the success of a significant transaction for a corporate client that the researcher would be brought "over the wall." This immediately froze the analyst from any further public commentary or disclosure on the company in question until the transaction was announced publicly and the information was no longer considered proprietary. It was a great honor for an analyst to be brought over the wall.

I had begun to feel that Dana was becoming distant and distracted as her career took flight. A brief dinner we had shared at a popular new restaurant had only compounded my concerns. While we talked over the succulent red snapper in a sweet onion vinegar marinade that both of us had ordered, Dana looked tired and troubled. Although we didn't finish dinner until after ten o'clock that night, she ordered a double espresso and announced that she was on her way back to the office. "Duty calls," she had chirped with a counterfeit joy, oblivious to my obvious disappointment. It had been a while since I had been asked to visit her and my freshly dry-cleaned and laundered clothes in Hoboken.

I thought if I could persuade her to leave the city for a couple of days, I could coax her back into a more playful—and more affectionate—mood and give her a break from what was evidently an intoxicating, but all-consuming, assignment.

But when I called Dana, an exasperated voice answered her phone line on the third ring and sighed heavily when I asked to speak with her.

"No. Not today, Mr. Perkins. Not even this week. She is out. Gone." I hung up without leaving a message.

I wondered whether it was only work that was consuming her. It occurred to me that perhaps she had become bored with her boyfriend from Kansas.

∽

The spiny mass of shifting rock and sand known as Cape Cod has long been favored by people seeking to escape the tribulations of society, especially in the off-season when summer was over. It is a place dimpled by kettle ponds and tidal marshes formed by ancient glaciers, a place of pristine natural seashore and secluded dead-end roads nestled among the trees. In the summer its sun-splashed beaches and brightly festooned Main Street shops smile broadly with the clutter of pleasure seekers. But after the final leaves of autumn drift off their perches and the urbanites abandon their playground to the locals, the Cape shows its moody side. The surf chews at the empty stretches of sand, and the wind blows cantankerously across the land. The fishing boats return to empty piers, and reclusive retirees wander out of their hideaways to watch the angry sea. When the Cape skies turn dark and turbulent, only the steady beacon of the cliffside lighthouse and the twinkle of lanterns in the shore road inn serve as reminders that there are still people, light, and warmth here.

As I crossed the Sagamore Bridge and entered the nearly desolate main artery that runs from the Cape Cod Canal all the way to the tip of the Outer Cape at Provincetown, I pondered the curious turn of events that had dispatched me to this place. I rolled down the window to taste and breathe the liberating sting of salty ocean air. For the first time in a long while, I felt free from the clutches of a dangerous destiny. It was a feeling I had hoped to share with Dana. With one hand on the wheel, I unfolded the map on which I had carefully marked my route. The four-lane road suddenly narrowed to two lanes, and I continued on for several miles before taking an exit road that led to a meandering roadway with scenic views along the edge of the deceptively docile Atlantic Ocean. A gilt-edged gray sky was giving way to darkening shades of blue when I turned into the gravel parking lot of a small inn with a "Rooms Available" sign in the office window. I went to bed early without eating and slept deeply, despite my empty stomach.

The ocean was churning and growling when I checked out early the next morning. I drove slowly along the shore road until it twisted toward Main Street of a quaint town. My first stop was the hardware store. Strolling in with the confidence of a local contractor, rolling up my sleeves and twisting the baseball cap on my head, I picked up the first bulky item I could find, which happened to be a paint sprayer.

Ambling up to the counter, which was attended by a middle-aged woman with a high hairdo and granny glasses, I blustered, "Gotta deliver this to Leonard Colesmith. Can you tell me the address?" Peering over her spectacles, the woman slowly surveyed me from top to bottom before staring me directly in the eyes.

"No. I cannot. Will you be paying cash or credit?" I had received my firsthand tutorial on the insularity of the *Cape-Coddahs*.

Tossing my useless hardware purchase into the backseat of the car I had parked on the curbside of the mostly deserted street, I looked up and down for my next opportunity. I spied the brick façade of a small public library. This time, I would be a little more inventive in my approach. Slinking through the front doors, I quickly ducked behind a high bookshelf. I piled my arms ridiculously high with a stack of books, carefully removing the checkout cards from each of them and stuffing them in my pocket. Then I glanced toward the checkout desk to ensure that I would not be observed approaching from behind the bookshelf area. Seeing that the desk was unattended and the library practically empty, I bolted toward the front door and then turned sharply as if I had just arrived to return an overflowing collection of borrowed tomes. Struggling noisily and with great effort, I plopped my stack heavily on the counter just as a librarian emerged from a room behind the checkout counter.

"Oh, my word—let me help you with that," she exclaimed.

"Thank you, thank you very much," I sighed. "Mr. Colesmith has asked me to return these on his behalf."

"Colesmith? Lenny? Really?" She looked confused. "Well—okay then—I will get to this shortly. Thank you for bringing them in."

"Well—actually—given the number of volumes, he wanted me to stay to see that all of the books were marked 'returned.' I really apologize for the inconvenience."

The round, pink-cheeked librarian was flustered, but eventually she turned to retrieve an index-sized piece of paper from a file drawer behind her and then turned her attention toward the high stack of books I had placed in front of her. Her brow wrinkled, and she leaned closer to what was evidently Colesmith's library card.

"Now, this is indeed strange," she said as she ran her finger along the spine of the tower of books.

"What is it?" I leaned in against the counter and gently, but confidently, pulled the library card toward me in one sweeping motion. Immediately I understood the librarian's confusion. Other than his name, phone number, and street address, the library card was blank. In an instant, I was on my way out the door.

"That is very strange, indeed," I called over my shoulder. "So sorry to have troubled you."

After a quick review of my map, I was again on my way, now within reach of my destination. The shore road took me to an obscure side street that led through a landscape of scrub pine and bayberry bushes. The road rose sharply to a promontory and ended in front of a magnificent gray- shingled house with blue shutters and sweeping views from its porches and windows of Pleasant Bay and the ocean beyond.

Before I had time to step out of the car, a figure appeared at the side porch. He took a few steps and then stopped. From my vantage point in the driver's seat, it seemed as though his reaction to my arrival was neutral, if somewhat wary. I scrambled to attention, got out of the car, and walked toward the stork-like figure, stretching my hand out in front of me, as much like a person walking in the dark as a polite stranger offering a greeting. A man with a handsome, weathered face, thinned by age, was studying me intently.

"You are Nathaniel—from the phone call?" I wasn't sure whether the voice reflected anger or anguish. "I had a feeling that you would come, following our conversation. I cannot say I am pleased...perhaps I am intrigued," he said without any note of emotion. "Come inside."

I followed Leonard Colesmith into a room with panoramic vistas of the water below. The tranquility of the lofty ocean views was trumped by an unexpected color chaos. Dramatic hues of deep burgundy and lime green spun around me like a pinwheel of colors while an assemblage of discordant furniture styles rested anxiously on a random interplay of carpets, wood, and tile; colored glass lamps were perched on tabletops sprinkled randomly throughout the cluttered space. I pushed aside a handful of finely crafted pillows and, at Colesmith's gesture of invitation, sat on a sofa upholstered in a crazy quilt. The house had the air of a hippy den. He might be retired, but he evidently hadn't allowed himself to be absorbed into the New England shabby chic of the typical Cape Cod beach home.

"I understand from our brief telephone conversation that you are working for Lucas Orr at the *Tantalus Fund*," Colesmith said, speaking slowly and deliberately, as though he were a lawyer making a case. "Let me make a surmise, then. You are increasingly uncomfortable about something that you cannot really put your finger on? Hmm?" Colesmith leaned toward me, squinting quizzically. He was awaiting an explanation for my blatant intrusion despite his refusal to see or talk to me. I wasn't sure why he had even allowed me to enter his house unless I was a diversion from a too-quiet life.

"It's not that I can put my finger on any particular concern or impropriety as such, but...there is...you know the feeling you get when you are hanging onto a rope and then your grip begins slowly to slip?" I was stammering out an unrehearsed speech, and I knew that Colesmith needed to hear more before responding.

"Continue," he said bluntly.

"The way we operate, sort of on that thin edge that separates brilliance from malevolence, is making me nervous. You should understand that we do great work as investors, we really do, but the way we prey on the human element is vicious, maybe even diabolical."

"And...?" Colesmith was goading me, wanting more.

"And here is the thing," I continued. "I sort of fell into this place, without much deliberation, actually. I thought it was going to be a dream job. Now the one person I trusted is gone, and I am feeling exposed. Lucas Orr would not approve of my being here, as I'm sure you can imagine, but I am doing what he trained me to do—seeking answers."

The older man rubbed his eyes for several minutes as if reflecting on a life lost. When he looked at me, I noticed sadness in his expression.

"Why should I trust you? Are you a masked emissary from Luc?" he asked, and then he answered himself. "No, there's nothing he wants from me anymore," he mumbled. Then he began to speak more forcefully.

"Orr was the most brilliant mind I ever encountered in the business," Colesmith said, staring into space as he spoke.

"I hired him to manage the back office of our trading operations, but he quickly insinuated himself into our investment process. He would labor long nights for weeks on end, studying the financial statements of the companies we were invested in. Then he would walk into my office with a crisp analysis demonstrating *without a doubt* that a certain company was plumping its earnings by capitalizing costs that should have been expensed, or that a different company was heavily exposed to soaring commodity costs. We would sell the stock, and invariably it would later plunge in value."

Colesmith lowered his gaze to address me directly. "The funny thing was, Orr only had a penchant for the contrary, for the dark side of things. He was an oracle in the world of negativity."

"Yes, that's true," I said eagerly, urging Colesmith to go on.

"I had no choice but to promote him—he was so valuable to the firm. But fairly quickly, the dynamic changed. It was no longer me giving, but Orr taking. As his profits swelled, his authority became similarly engorged. I was powerless in the very firm I had created. And his methods...his methods were indeed distasteful." The words were coming at a faster clip now.

"Through means only he knew, Orr developed a conduit that gave him knowledge of the trading flows inside Farragut Funds, the mammoth mutual fund complex. That firm used to trade ten percent of the volume of all shares on the New York Stock Exchange in the old days, so knowing whether they were selling oil stocks or buying banks could be very valuable information, indeed. He knew I disapproved of using knowledge gained in that fashion for our own trading advantage, but he continued apace and the profits poured into our thriving enterprise." He paused and then spit out a condemnation.

"Money is like seawater—the more you drink, the thirstier you get." I could not tell if he was referring to himself or to his onetime protégé.

"What happened?" I asked.

"Something had to give." Colesmith sighed, expelling a long release of oxygen. "It turned out to be me. One day Orr and Ashton Malpas walked into my office and handed me a separation agreement. The deal was that I would agree to a large cash payment and surrender my ownership of the firm to Orr. And they made sure that I was aware that they knew all my secrets. The gall of it was that Malpas, my trusted junior partner, did all the talking. It was an unemotional ultimatum delivered with the precision of an executioner's bullet. They had the power."

"I'm sorry," I said. I realized that I was extending an apology for something that happened long ago, when I still thought of Wall Street the way Bull Wertz had imagined it—as controlled by men of brilliance and integrity.

"There's more," Colesmith said. "I had left the company, but I was still living in New York when I heard that Luc and Malpas were in an awkward situation. Malpas had a beautiful wife. She came from somewhere in the Middle East, spoke five languages, and worked as an interpreter at the United Nations. She fell under Luc's spell and walked out on Malpas to move in with Luc. The astonishing part of the story is that Luc and Malpas continued to work together as though nothing had happened. I don't know how it turned out between Luc and the woman. I remember her; she was a stunner, smart but soft. Can't remember her name."

Colesmith finished this astonishing tale by mumbling, as if speaking to himself, "You know what they say...if you want a friend on Wall Street, get a dog."

"Jasmin," I said. "Was her name Jasmin?"

"Might be," Colesmith answered. "Some kind of flower anyway. Fragrant." He laughed. "Night-blooming jasmine."

Then Colesmith returned to my question. "If you want to know what makes Luc Orr the kind of man he is, I can't tell you. I never understood him myself. Why have you come so far to find out?"

In an instant I was unleashing my dreams and apprehensions to this stranger in the spectacularly eccentric seaside house. I told him about Kansas, Bull Wertz, and my brief career at Platt Brothers. I held nothing back, and I spoke without interruption. When I came to Orr, my breathless narrative stopped.

"I mean, what kind of place is Wall Street that no one trusts anyone else? Even my girlfriend doesn't trust me enough to tell me what she's doing—and of course I have pledged an oath of secrecy to tell no one what I am working on at Tantalus. And while we are all so focused on protecting our own secrets, everyone else is hard at work trying to ferret us out."

Colesmith smiled broadly. "Don't you see that your search for me—prosecuted through whatever unscrupulous methods you have seen fit to employ—has elegantly embraced the very snooping culture that supposedly makes you unsettled?"

I was embarrassed that the thought had not occurred to me, and I felt diminished by the revelation.

"Ah, well, if Luc hired you and has given you enough responsibility that you are beginning to feel uncomfortable, you must be a promising young man. Maybe you can avoid turning into him."

Then he stood to indicate that the interview was over. He had not offered me so much as a glass of water although he knew I had traveled hundreds of miles to meet him.

"Thank you," I said.

"Of course, I haven't solved the puzzle for you, and I doubt anyone can, but that is where my story ends." Then, jolted by a reminder, he excused himself and strode into an adjoining room that appeared to serve as an office. I could see him bend over to open a file drawer and pick out a thick, manila envelope. Then he came back and handed it to me.

"There is also this—old securities portfolios, client lists, and miscellaneous documents from the long-deceased Colesmith Capital. It probably won't help you, but I certainly don't have any further use for it."

That was all. Colesmith ushered me to the door, and as I retreated to my car through the gathering dusk, I turned to glance back at him, standing where I had left him, a subdued man in a big house.

The return trip to New York seemed to take much longer than the five hours driving north. When I arrived at my apartment well after nightfall, the first thing I noticed was a solitary red blip on my answering machine. The voice I heard when I pressed the button was haunting after our conversation only a couple of days earlier. It was Malpas.

147

"Be in Luc's office at seven in the morning. The big hunt is on." I stood, dazed, for several minutes before shuffling off to bed. The knowledge that I had been tapped to enter Orr's circle of confidence on an important new undertaking made me shudder, partly with excitement, but also with fear. At home in Kansas, I had often shot partridge and thought of myself as a competent hunter. But I never shot more than I ate or could give away to friends. Now I was wondering if I wasn't really a hunter after all.

CHAPTER EIGHT

Shortly after his son George's death, Commodore Vanderbilt became inflamed with his most acute, most transformational business insight. Having concluded that the steamship business was too crowded and competitive, with waterways open to all comers afloat, he divested himself of the bulk of his shipping interests. Foreseeing a sharp decline in waterborne commerce in favor of overland transportation, Vanderbilt moved aggressively into railroads. He had dabbled in railroads since the 1840s, accepting directorships and extending credit, mainly as a means of supporting the through-transit of his shipping interests. Now he recognized that, unlike the waterways, rail lines were innately structured to have a natural, built-in buffer against competition—the tracks and the routes—and furthermore, they were subsidized by the government, which gave many of the rail lines the land surrounding the tracks as well.

The great railroad men would soon monopolize the point-to-point transit of goods, and Vanderbilt was intent on joining their ranks. For some railroad pioneers, building the roads represented the romance of opening new, untouched parts of the country to settlement and commerce. For the Commodore, railroads were just another business.

We gathered around our leader like a pack of wolves. Lucas Orr stood behind his imposing desk, implacable and confident, and we sat waiting. In addition to me, the assembly included

Ashton Malpas and two others. A fresh-faced recent recruit tapped his feet while a faded, rumpled form—whose function was undefined, but who, it would turn out, knew whom to call and how to ask the right questions—sat inert next to him. Malpas was hunched over a notepad, seated furthest from Orr, and for the first time I realized that no matter how closely they worked together, Malpas kept the maximum distance between them, and they rarely made eye contact. Orr rose above us, and foreboding shivers ran over me as he spoke.

"We have met face-to-face with powerful enemies before. We have proved their vulnerabilities and have remained resolute in the face of malice as these targets have ultimately succumbed to our quest for truth. But never before today have we challenged a force whose tentacles of power extend so broadly and whose instinct for survival will trample all rules of fair play. We will need to be at our best. And I must know that each of you stand with me, unwaveringly." Lucas Orr paused, as though waiting for the questions that he knew would not come. He continued.

"First, a brief lesson regarding this assignment." Orr assumed the demeanor of a tutor looking down on his pupils.

"The crucial variable driving our society's technology revolution is the ability to pack data more and more densely into smaller and smaller devices. This has allowed us to shrink the computing power of massive mainframe computers onto a person's desktop." Orr's audience listened with rapt attention.

"Then we shrank the massive processing power again to fit into a small machine that could sit on our laps. And we will shrink it again and again over time to fit into the palm of our hand and ultimately into a space no bigger than the face of a wristwatch. This process of technological progress has been enshrined in a doctrine termed Moore's Law, which stipulates that the data capacity of a silicon chip doubles roughly every eighteen months." Orr shimmered with his own kind of electricity leaving no doubt that he was passionate about the quest ahead.

"Whole industries have been built around the power of Moore's Law. One product after another—computers, automobiles, appliances, and consumer electronics—has become faster, cheaper, and smarter. Wave after wave of innovation has flowed over every industry in America as one advance in computing power has been leapfrogged by the next. It has been said that the resulting technology boom has led to the largest legal creation of wealth in history. But the stakes are very, very high for those companies that play in this fast-changing terrain. One company's breakthrough can mean another company's demise." I sensed that we were about to descend from this summit of inspiration into the murky hollows where my next assignment lurked.

Orr smiled without showing his teeth, his hands flapping strangely at his sides as if he were casting a spell. But his entire demeanor radiated strength.

"Quotient Corporation is quickly becoming a household name as an enabler of the tech revolution. The fawning press even refers to this company as *the IBM of a new generation*."

Orr paused as someone among us silently caught his breath. I felt my ears reddening as I pondered Orr's audacity—we had set our sights on an icon of American industry! Over the past several years, Quotient Corporation and its executives had probably been featured on the covers of *Forbes* and *Time* magazines more frequently than the leaders of any company in America. Everyone had heard of the company's extraordinary MicroMagnet, a miniaturized data capture disk that allowed for the storage and retrieval of data at a transfer rate far faster than any competing technologies. Nearly every major laptop computer maker and cell phone manufacturer had licensed the MicroMagnet for use in their products. Quotient had quickly become the only game in town; everyone needed a MicroMagnet because any manufacturer that had a reputation for high latency, otherwise known as slow loading speed, would quickly be out of business. Enormous pricing power flowed from this competitive advantage, and Quotient's profits had skyrocketed.

"As the sizeable profits have ballooned, this bounty has not only been reinvested in the research required to sustain the company's lead, but," and he lowered his voice, "the riches have also leached into the pockets of powerful people in lofty places. Congressmen, senators, and governors are greatly indebted to Quotient for large contributions to their parties and their personal campaigns. Quotient has also made bargains of one sort and another with key regulators who govern anticompetitive business practices and who turn a blind eye to the scorching tactics the company uses against its competitors." Orr was grinning now as though, by simply having the nerve to take on Quotient, he had already won the first round. "This will be no easy foe."

Orr stopped and looked around the room at each of us. When it was clear that he had finished talking, we all stood to leave. His operation was so well organized that we knew what we would be expected to do and how we should instruct others to support our efforts. The eager recruit would pull every financial document that Quotient Corporation had filed since they had become a public company. He would scrutinize financial ratios and footnotes and legal disclosures for any red flag that might signal a point of vulnerability. The quiet, rumpled guy would work a different angle, tracking down former employees and customers and competitors, seeking anecdotes and rumors that might lead our platoon to an exposed underbelly of the beast. Malpas would remain inscrutable, and I would work directly with Orr on special assignments.

"Nate, you can stay," Orr said before I crossed the threshold. I returned to my seat in front of the master, awaiting a revelation that Orr had decided not to share broadly.

"We are in a race against time," Orr said matter-of-factly. Then, giving no hint that he was revealing privileged information, he continued.

"Within the next two weeks, Quotient will be filing a registration statement to sell over a billion dollars of stock. The SEC will review the documents ever so briefly and quickly approve the sale of these shares to the public. About half the money will go toward bolstering the company's war chest for research and development, new factories, and to batter their competitors in the marketplace." Orr paused.

"Who gets the rest of the loot?" I asked.

"Crouse & Potter is the venture capital firm that originally funded the company, and they still own 25 percent of the shares. They will be selling half their remaining stake in this offering. Perhaps Claude Potter needs to build another fifty-room mansion," Orr said, his voice rising uncharacteristically. I thought he was beginning to sound almost delirious.

"So let me be clear," I mustered. "We will be taking on one of the nation's most admired young companies, the Securities and Exchange Commission, the top venture capitalist firm in America, and powerful members of the United States Senate?" I had a vision of myself as an ensign in the British Army, commissioned to carry the flag into battle and to suffer certain death at the first volleys of enemy gunfire.

Orr smiled. "Correct. But they don't know what I know."

In the early part of the twentieth century, the mighty New York Central Railroad embarked on a visionary project that forever altered the streetscape of New York's grandest boulevard. Expending vast sums of capital, the city's main rail terminal and its busy network of surrounding train tracks were relocated from street level to below ground. With the bellow and bedlam of a busy rail yard sealed in her subterranean chamber, majestic structures rose on the strategically-placed lots in architectural majesty on the renewed Park Avenue. Members of a well-known New York family, the Astors, owned some of the key real estate above the newly subterranean rail lines, and they built an imposing new structure on an entire block from Forty-ninth to Fiftieth Street, a structure that, perhaps more than any other of its kind, redefined the image of the American hotel. No longer merely a place of accommodation for weary transients, the grand city hotel became a place of luxury and elegance, with bars and restaurants where the titans of commerce would mingle and connive.

The Waldorf-Astoria was no longer unique or even particularly exclusive, but it was still grand, and it had remained a tourist attraction. A flow of humanity strolled and browsed the shops in her lobby, admiring her classic luxuriance. The lighting was soft, the furniture a mixture of Gilded Age and Art Deco, and the carpeting plush.

It was there that Luc had sent me for a critical meeting. I headed for the focal point of the lobby, a nine-foot clock encircled with bronze plaques depicting the images of seven U.S. presidents and Queen Victoria. The man I had been directed to look for, whom I knew only as "Azam," stood just to the side of the clock. He wore a perfectly fitted black suit and a vest with shiny buttons. He was slender and swarthy, but he was also close-shaven and manicured, and he emanated the faux elegance particular to certain senior hotel employees. I nodded at him twice, he nodded back, and then he turned to walk across the great open space as I followed. En route, he paused several times to greet distinguished visitors, seated in groups of chairs and sofas, conveying the familiarity of a long-serving fixture of the famous hotel. As I watched the interplay, I recognized the rosy, round face and balding pate of one of America's most prominent CEOs. I had seen his photograph often; he had a big head, but he was much shorter than I had expected.

Azam appeared to serve in an official guest service function, somewhere between manager and concierge at this sumptuous crossroads of wealth. He seemed a throwback to a time when hotel managers were called on to arrange for the discreet delivery of girls or booze to the politicians, titans, gangsters, and socialites who were among the Waldorf's clientele. Azam opened the door and waved me into a small private room, quickly closing the door behind us.

"The guest you are looking for can be found in a room on the fourteenth floor. His wife has gone to a Broadway play and will not return until close to midnight." Azam smiled at me in a way that made me think of carnivores and implied the confidence of hidden knowledge. His teeth were perfectly aligned, but their tips were pointed.

"Is there anything else?" I asked.

"If the gentleman should make any difficulties, Mr. Orr has suggested that you might mention an intimate knowledge of what transpired in his hotel room during his visit of March 1986," he said.

As I left the small chamber tucked into the recesses of the magnificent edifice, I marveled that even this man was an obscure appendage of Lucas Orr's power. I doubted that they taught Azam's skills in the management program at the Cornell School of Hotel Administration.

When I knocked sharply on the door of a suite at the end of a long hallway of the Waldorf-Astoria, two days had elapsed since I had received my original instructions from Lucas Orr. In the intervening period, I had studied diligently and was now a forty-eight-hour expert on medical ailments afflicting workers in the high-tech industry. I had read the testimony in a big IBM case regarding allegations of an elevated incidence of cancer among the employees of their semiconductor manufacturing operations. I had pored over the leading studies on mortality rates from long-term exposure to toxic resins used for coating microchips. And I had learned as much as I could about the dangers of sustained exposure to electromagnetic fields.

At room 1412, a squat, plump man wearing the hotel's terrycloth bathrobe promptly opened the door. He barely greeted me before he led me to a small table in the corner of the room and pointed. I pulled up a chair, sat, and leafed through a short stack of papers that were dense with tables, charts, and figures.

"It's all there," the man said curtly. "Quotient Corporation's dirty little secret. We became aware pretty early on that the innovative manufacturing technique we had perfected to pack the data within a billionth of a second was also creating very dangerous EMFs, electromagnetic fields. We had never before registered EMFs on this scale."

I tilted my head to indicate that he should continue.

"As an early precaution, it was decided that we should start keeping records of the long-term health effects on workers who were most closely involved in the manufacturing process. Naturally, these records were very closely guarded and known to only a very small handful of employees. If anyone asked if we had been keeping records, it would have been denied absolutely." The man sighed.

"And?"

"As you will see, the results are terrible—brain tumors, leukemia, liver, pituitary gland. As I said, it's all there." He looked at me with an expression that was part sorrow and part angry disdain.

"Look, I don't know who you guys are or how you found me. I don't want to know. But I have now delivered what I promised, and your pledge is to leave me alone and never contact me again. I am retired. I am done with all this. And my wife will be home from the theatre soon. So please leave."

I packed the papers into my briefcase and left room 1412. As I made my way down the plush, carpeted hallway, I marveled at Lucas Orr's ability to crack open valuable sources the way a shucker opens an oyster, with a swift twist of a sharp blade. I also realized that I had barely spoken a word during my meeting with the man in the bathrobe.

The next morning, I presented the secret documents to Orr.

"We have it," I said proudly.

But he snapped back, "We have nothing. There is a big difference between knowing where gold lies and getting it out of the ground, between conceiving of something and executing it." He paused. "Our work has only just begun." I flushed, like a pupil who had just been scolded by his teacher.

"Tell me what you have learned about Crouse & Potter," Orr demanded, moving on to another phase of my assignment. After several days of study, I felt like an historian of the legendary venture capital firm.

"Daniel Crouse and Claude Potter are widely regarded as the pioneers of the modern venture capital industry. They established one of the first independent firms in 1972, on Sand Hill Road in Menlo Park, the stretch of orange-groves-turned-office parks in the heart of Silicon Valley." The term had become synonymous with the venture capital industry and had emerged as a headquarters location for many of the world's top financiers.

"In earlier days, speculative start-up enterprises were typically funded by wealthy individuals and families. CP organized a limited partnership structure where individuals and institutions put up the capital and a small team of investment professionals managed the investments as general partners, in return for a 1 percent management fee and 20 percent of the profits."

"I know all that," Orr said impatiently as I continued.

"CP's launch coincided with a boom in technology innovation. The firm was perfectly positioned to fund some of the most successful new companies in the electronics, computer hardware, and software industries. The profits from their ownership stakes made each of the top partners worth hundreds of millions of dollars. It isn't hard to see why this limited partnership model has been emulated by a whole new generation of leveraged buyout specialists and hedge fund managers."

Orr had been leaning back in his chair, eyes closed, apparently lost in thought. He sat upright and made a circling gesture with his hand to indicate that I should speed up and get to the point.

"You are getting off course. Talk to me about Crouse and Potter, the people."

"Daniel Crouse and Claude Potter had the perfect combination of skills. Crouse was the smooth-talking financial guy, a banker by training, who had financed many of the leading technology companies in the Bay area. Potter was the awkward, unkempt scientist who spent many years in the research labs of Xerox and moved on to their Palo Alto Research Center before teaming up with Crouse. The breadth of their relationships in finance and industry immediately stamped CP as the top brand for the most worthy entrepreneurs. Their success was built on that rare situation: partners who complement rather than compete with each other," I said. I was thinking about Orr and Leonard Colesmith as I spoke.

"What else do you know of the individuals?" Orr asked.

"Daniel Crouse has always been the more public of the two partners...sort of a bon vivant bachelor who lives in San Francisco. Crouse became chairman emeritus last year, so he has stepped down from active involvement in the firm's investment activities. In fact, he has been trekking in Asia for the past six months."

"And Potter?" Orr was leaning toward me with more eagerness than he usually displayed.

"Claude Potter is a sphinx; he appears to make up for his deficit of charm with a surplus of cash. He is intensely private, never gives interviews, and lives in a walled compound. He is reputed to run the firm with an iron fist, making all the key decisions and serving on the boards of ten different portfolio companies and a few charitable foundations as well...made a fifty-million-dollar gift to Stanford last year. He is married to a prominent United States senator, but she goes by her maiden name, and the public at large rarely makes the connection. Evidently, the Potters don't connect a lot either. The senator spends most of her time in a charming brick Georgetown house."

I had exhausted my checklist, so I paused. Orr was adrift in meditation. I waited. After several minutes, he spoke.

"Our opponent is well armored, and his reputation will parry our most obvious line of attack. We don't have any hope with the major news organs. The *New York Times* and *Wall Street Journal* sit on their imperious thrones as the barons of what is newsworthy, and I doubt either of them will touch our controversial discovery with a ten-foot-pole, for fear of litigation as well as the potential loss of advertising from the phalanx of CP-affiliated entities. And the way Potter runs his firm, we won't find any weak links from inside the organization—perhaps Crouse, but we don't have time for that. Without a credible mouthpiece, our bombshell might just as well be counterfeit." Orr was talking aloud to himself.

"There will be rumors, mumbled in hushed tones over the years, but CP's monster will blaze on to greater profits and glory. They will ultimately resolve these serious problems with the safety of Quotient Corporation's innovative science, but they will do it slowly, on their terms, over time, and they will never recognize the long trail of suffering that they created in the process...unless..."

The way that Orr uttered "unless" chilled me. The two syllables hung over me like dread in the night.

CHAPTER NINE

In 1863 Cornelius Vanderbilt assumed control of the New York and Harlem Railroad and, after greasing the skids with the power brokers who controlled New York's Common Council, was granted a franchise to extend a streetcar service from Forty-second Street to the tip of Manhattan. Plotting against Vanderbilt and the surging share price of the Harlem line, one of the Commodore's business rivals cooked up a scheme, with the support of the aldermen of the Common Council, to sell short shares in the Harlem line. The Council planned to revoke the franchise to operate the streetcar line, even as Vanderbilt had begun to tear up the streets and lay rail. The plotters quickly filled out their short positions, expecting a handsome profit in the share price collapse that would surely follow when the city franchise was reclaimed.

But when that negative news was announced, the price of the Harlem stock did not drop for long. In fact, it slowly began to rise. Too late, the conspirators realized that Vanderbilt himself had bought up the entire floating supply of Harlem shares, "cornering the market," in the parlance of stock manipulators. As the short sellers panicked, the share price more than doubled. Vanderbilt, the pragmatic businessman, allowed the cornered short sellers, including certain of the aldermen, to cover their shares at a reduced loss in exchange for reinstating his franchise. The Commodore had scored a profit of many millions and had written a new chapter in the barbarous scrum of New York's financial markets.

❦

In a Washington, DC, cubicle with a view of Union Station, a middle-aged family man who commuted to the office every day from a three-bedroom ranch-style home in the Virginia suburbs sat poring over a legal document that had recently been placed into his in-box. It was a prospectus for a proposed offering of common stock for Quotient Corporation, and it had been marked with a small blue pencil check in the upper right hand corner of the cover page. There was no ambiguity about what this meant in the Division of Corporate Finance at the Securities and Exchange Commission. A check mark on the upper right cover page indicated a "marked filing," signifying that the issuer should be granted an accelerated review. Quotient's prospectus, the key disclosure document that was required to accompany the public placement of stock in the U.S. financial markets, would fly through the SEC with minimal changes. Quotient Corporation had friends in high places.

For several weeks, Orr was eerily silent on the subject of Quotient; he hadn't mentioned the name to me once. But one morning, he poked his head into my office and asked, "Do you know who won the bake-off for Quotient?" The "bake-off," an expression oddly reminiscent of a 1950s state fair, was a term used to describe the competition in which companies selected investment bankers to lead their stock offerings. In the case of landmark transactions like the Quotient deal, there would be a frenzy of bankers up and down Wall Street competing for the right to earn the plump fees that such an assignment would produce.

I had been calling my contacts around the Street looking for news or rumors about the pending stock offering. While

I had not come up with a definitive answer as a result of this approach, I told him what I had gleaned.

"At Platt Brothers, the deal is code-named Project Paramount, and the lead investment banker on their pitch team was marlin fishing in Cabo with Potter as recently as May."

"That's a start...what else?" Orr asked.

"Quotient has invited three firms to the beauty contest for the selection of lead underwriter. It's my understanding that the final word is going to be Potter's and Potter's alone. But I'm fairly certain Platt has it." I delivered my findings with the proud bearing of a studied apprentice. Orr was smiling.

I had discovered Platt's role by accident. One late night, Dana had called and asked if I could come over. Given the strange tinge of sadness in her voice and the strain which had developed of late in our relationship, I was eager to comply. By the time I had arrived, Dana had already fallen back asleep. She must have forgotten that she had left a marked-up and coffee-stained preliminary version of the Quotient registration document on her bedside table. The Platt Brothers name had been boldly displayed on the bottom left corner of the front page, indicating that the firm would play the role of lead underwriter of the transaction. At first I had tried to look away from the telltale confidential document. But lying clearly out in the open, the stapled sheaf of paper was like an entrancing flame, and I was drawn to it almost hypnotically. In the morning when we woke up, I had mentioned my discovery.

"Quotient, eh?" I blurted out. "Whew! This is the kind of blockbuster deal that could make your career, Dana." The tradition of Wall Street analysts wrapping themselves in the glow of a successful public offering was a well-trodden path to fame and financial success.

"You know that you aren't supposed to see that," Dana had snapped in response. "This deal isn't public yet." Dana was probably as angry at herself for leaving the document out as she was at me for looking at it. This was the woman I loved, and I briefly considered revealing my own secret, the role that I was playing in Lucas Orr's opposing blueprint for Quotient Corporation. If the Tantalus plan succeeded, it was likely to undermine Dana's professional aspirations. I was marching into war against the woman who had represented my emotional refuge and my comfort. Yet I had signed a confidentiality agreement, Lucas Orr was my boss, Tantalus was my employer, and I had my own career to consider. So I said nothing.

"We should have a public announcement of the final details of the transaction any day now because they want this deal on the fast track," I told Orr. "I think the road show will actually start in a week. I know that because the ballroom of the Hilton is reserved next Wednesday by Platt Brothers for a certain Project Paramount." Reporting what I had discovered gave me a momentary jolt of adrenaline, fueled by the narcotic of proprietary knowledge.

"Very good...stay on it," Orr said, although he knew the instruction was unnecessary.

When the press release was issued, announcing that Quotient had filed to sell one billion dollars of stock with Platt Brothers as lead manager of the deal, the markets buzzed with excitement. It was rightly assumed that this offering would be waved through the SEC and would hit the market very quickly. In an atypical response, Quotient's shares actually rose in price when the news of the pending offering was made public. Even recent business school graduates understood that the marketing process for the offering would unleash a torrent of new bullish expectations regarding the firm's prospects. The syndicate desk at Platt Brothers, the group responsible for managing the marketing process for the deal, would now shift to center stage. Their job was simple enough: orchestrate a road show that created more demand for shares than supply.

The road show was an updated financial version of the revival tent meetings of an earlier day when a preacher and his accomplices traveled in a caravan from one small town to the next, touting religion. In the modern version, company executives and their investment bankers toured the nation's key financial centers by private plane, selling what Andrew Carnegie called "The Gospel of Wealth." The financial road show aimed for high-minded intellectual engagement between the providers and the users of capital, but the potential buyers of stock were typically less interested in their own assessment of an investment than in how excited the competing buyers in the market were by the deal. If demand exceeded supply, that would translate into an immediate "pop" in aftermarket trading.

New York and Boston would be the centerpiece of a compressed, one-week marketing program for the Quotient road show. Platt would orchestrate the lunch meetings in large hotel banquet rooms, where the syndicate managers would be certain to instruct that the hotel set fewer seats than the number of confirmed attendees. That would create a noisy scramble as the presentation began, while testy waiters slapped down the missing place settings, and the guests were squeezed in, elbow-to-elbow. After that bit of theater, the investors would return to their offices with the distinct impression that the marketplace was clamoring to get a piece of the deal. And in short order, the marketplace would know for sure that the Quotient deal was "hot."

In its haste to do the deal, the Quotient road show would skip over the largely ceremonial visits to investors in London and on the Continent, where tradition held that the company management—and their accompanying spouses—would spend more time shopping than selling. The show would, however, include a brief stopover in a suburb northwest of Milwaukee, where a booming mutual fund firm had made a business practice of buying every bellwether new stock issue in large quantity, thus endearing themselves to the brokerage firms and assuring a steady access to future deal allocations.

I was quite certain that a new tab had been added to the green three-ringer binder that sat on Platt's syndicate desk, recording the book of investor demand. As the marketing process unfolded, the syndicate manager would surreptitiously add several large new orders to the book on behalf of fictional accounts so that when salespeople checked on the shape of the deal for their clients, the word would go out that interest was strong. Demand would feed demand, and in the final allocation of a successful deal, the fictional orders would simply disappear as if they had never existed.

During a late-morning lull in the caffeine-addled brains of the Platt Brothers stock department, my phone rang. Tom McGuire was on the other end. Evidently, the blustering salesman had concluded his morning pandering to his priority customers, and he had some time to kill. McGuire kicked back in fabricated geniality.

"Hey, Perk...guess which firm will be leading the biggest deal of the year?"

Since I already knew that Platt Brothers had been chosen to lead the billion-dollar Quotient stock offering, I steered the bombastic stock vendor to the question searing a hole inside me. I could almost hear the steady pulsing of my heart as I asked my question.

"Uh, yeah, I heard. Congrats. And which research analyst will be given the honor of peddling the deal?"

"It will be that dreamy piece of ass, the incognito heiress, Ms. Dana Rocca, of course. I heard from syndicate that she was the reason we won the mandate. She's a big star around here these days. And you can imagine how the client base will relish her calls and visits."

"Uh...sure." I said meekly.

Lowering his voice for effect, McGuire forged on. "They say she's got a mystery man on the outside, but she certainly knows how to titillate the masses." I could feel McGuire's leering presence oozing through the telephone line.

As I had seen Dana less than usual lately, while McGuire assumed I was the mystery man, I wasn't so sure. A deepening discomfort was choking off my ability to force out any speech, but I managed a parting shot.

"I gotta say—you certainly understand the art of selling stocks. Breasts and bluster. Hope for your sake that this never becomes an intellectual exercise, McGuire, or you will become as relevant as the Underwood typewriter."

The broad-bellied salesman grunted. "Ha, good one, Perk. Hey...I see Ms. Rocca is making the rounds up here on the sales floor right now. Do you want to have a quick chat with her on the Quotient deal?" Lowering his voice, McGuire sneered, "Cheaper than a 1-900 call." At that quip, I hung up.

I could no longer avoid the perception that something was very wrong. It lingered heavily, haunting me. I was surprised by the feeling, as if remembering something I had never known. It was a tingling awareness that Dana and I were being seduced and hunted by the same dark force. While I knew that Quotient was on a collision course with Tantalus, Dana believed it was the deal of a lifetime. As I rushed from the office like a man dropped overboard into a sea of cold water, Patrick raised his thick head to watch me. A stately Masonic grandfather clock with twin brass finials tolled noon when I scrambled through the exit door.

I meandered the New York streets for hours as the day faded and skyscrapers began to cast long shadows. The city was still in its spring mood, with warming days quickly bringing new energy to the streetscapes. I studied people as I roamed, thinking miserable thoughts. Even when I saw happy or contented expressions, I wondered what sorrows and broken dreams hid behind their false assurance. What clandestine indiscretions tormented even the perky and well-appointed passersby? I bumped awkwardly through the streets of my adopted town for hours, feeling alien and alone, not fully cognizant of where I was going.

At some point I looked up to realize that I was walking the streets of old New York. The narrow thoroughfares of a simpler time seemed strangely comforting as the towers of sculpted concrete, steel, and glass loomed above me, pressing in from my flanks. I ducked in from the alley behind Federal Hall and was standing at the fountainhead of American finance. Wall Street, famously described as a narrow, crooked street with the river at one end and a graveyard at the other, was thronged with the brightly-shirted clerks from the New York Stock Exchange, who mingled between scurrying businessmen and foreign tourists. I wandered over to the building at the southeast corner of Wall and Broad streets to look for the scarring from an infamous bombing of the J.P. Morgan building in 1920 that had killed scores of bystanders and maimed hundreds. Finally, I turned up the block toward Trinity Church, where I hailed a passing yellow cab, stumbled in at curbside, and blurted out my destination.

"Hoboken is double-meter," the cabbie stuttered in broken English. His front teeth were coffee-stained and chipped.

"Yeah, okay, sure." I nodded my assent and sat back for a ride through the tunnel that snaked beneath the Hudson

River, on my way to the narrow street of row houses where Dana lived. When we arrived, I realized that the grubby cabbie had charged me double-fare for the entire trip, instead of the proper accounting; he should have only charged me double for the portion of the trip outside Manhattan's boundaries. But I paid without dispute and ambled out to a street side café across the street from the entrance to Dana's apartment. I would wait for her to come home.

I sat there watching as the world wandered by—babies in strollers with mothers running late-day errands, schoolchildren frolicking in packs, and young professionals scurrying home after a densely-packed New York commute.

Sitting in silence as darkness fell, I watched a series of couples stroll by under the glow of a streetlamp. After I had consumed multiple large pints of increasingly tasteless beer, the waitress dropped the check on my table.

"Closing time, darling." She was a redhead with a fabulous toothy smile—broad-hipped and bouncy and full of life. She probably would make a fine wife for somebody.

"Boy, the time flies when I'm around you…" I stood unsteadily and made an awkward motion to hug her. She deftly deflected my approach and, with a one-handed sweep of her arm, turned me firmly toward the door.

"The pleasure has been all mine, darling," she chirped kindly. "Until we meet again."

Stumbling out into the street, I was alone again. There had been no sign of Dana entering her apartment building, and even if she had gone out to dinner, it was far later than she would normally return home. I walked across the one-way street, lined on both sides with tightly parked cars, and plopped down on her stoop to rest and wait. Shortly thereafter, the bouncy redhead walked by briskly on her way home after closing time. I caught her glancing at me sideways as she hurried past, a gaze that was quickly, embarrassedly, averted. Soon I was asleep.

I woke in that lost time between night and sunrise to a feeling of stiffness and melancholy. I understood that Dana would not be coming home, so I dusted myself off and wandered away to catch the early bus back to New York.

The best time to get a Wall Street executive on the telephone is that brief, unguarded window between the hour of their arrival and the time that the secretarial pool assembles at their workstations. At precisely 7:25 a.m., Dana picked up her phone on the second ring.

"Hi, it's me. I wasn't sure if you might be out of town," I said, as calmly as possible.

"Oh, hi," her voiced was light and mildly affectionate. "It's just work and home for me these days." Then there was a stillness that extended a little too long. "You know that I'm a slave until this Quotient deal gets done. I'm sorry, Nate, but that's the way it has to be."

I offered a meaningless parting comment before carefully placing the receiver back in its cradle, as though it was a fragile object that had to be handled very delicately. For several moments my mind spun in an accelerated and disorienting circle of emotions. Suddenly I bolted out of my chair and rushed toward Orr's office. I blamed him for everything that had ever gone wrong in my life—for Dana's distance, for my disillusionment—and in my secret heart, I wondered if Dana was a slave to Quotient, or if she had become a member of Orr's harem. I wanted to act out, throw myself savagely upon him, to inflict physical pain, to see whether his reaction would be that of a mortal man, or if he would still be as cool as he always was. I surged into his darkened suite. The high back of his desk chair was turned toward the door, and I couldn't tell if there was anyone sitting there. I spun the chair toward me, and it yielded easily. It was empty.

I turned from Orr's command center and dashed to the adjoining space where the lights were on. The broad face of Ashton Malpas turned up slowly to face me, and his expression broke into a smarmy smile.

"Yes, Nate. What is it?"

Before I had time to blurt out my rage, I heard the voice of Lucas Orr inside my head, counseling me.

"Nothing. It's nothing," I mumbled.

Slowly retreating to my own office, I collapsed into dazed contemplation. A sudden wailing of the telephone interrupted my thoughts. I waited, counting the rings. On the fifth chord, I picked up. My mother, breathless, announced herself.

"Mr. Wertz passed last night. There is a memorial service Wednesday. Do you think you could get time off to come home? I know he would have wanted you to speak. Can you be here?" My mind suddenly swept back across a thousand miles to the flat wheatlands where I had first become enchanted by Wall Street.

"Mr. Wertz? I didn't even know that he was sick."

"It was a particularly nasty form of cancer, and it happened quickly. Don't blame yourself, Nate; he didn't want people to know."

My first instinct had not necessarily been to feel guilty, but new waves of self-abhorrence swamped me. This formative early mentor, this amiable force of positive inspiration was now gone. It had been nearly a year since I had seen or spoken with him. Then, I was hopeful. Now I resided in the house of darkness and denial. I was glad he had never discovered what his beloved Wall Street could be like. "I will be there," I said.

CHAPTER TEN

Cornelius Vanderbilt was on an extended summer retreat at a fine hotel in Saratoga when he heard that Sophie, his wife of fifty-five years, had died after an extended illness. Vanderbilt had escaped to the "trotters" after suffering a humiliating setback in a long battle with Jay Gould and Jim Fisk to corner the shares of the Erie Railroad. Committing large sums of money to buy up the floating supply of stock while promulgating bullish commentary into the markets, the Commodore's well-established cornering scheme had backfired when Gould and Fisk had blatantly manufactured the issuance of new shares through secret votes of the company's board. Flooded with shares despite Vanderbilt's large purchases, the Erie stock price had tumbled in the face of confusion and uncertainty. In the end, Vanderbilt had lost seven million dollars. Chastened and embarrassed, he would never again stake his wealth in pursuit of a cornering play. Without fanfare, he handed the operating control of his vast business interests to his son William, the heir apparent to the Vanderbilt empire.

෴

Abilene, Kansas, is a place of wide skies and small homes located in the flatlands about a two-hour drive west of Kansas City. For a town of only several thousand residents, it has a lot of history. Abilene was the terminus of a dirt road that stretched from the southern Texas ranches, a passage that came to be known as the Chisholm Trail. There, cattle that had been pushed overland for hundreds of miles were inventoried and traded to the local stockyards. Shipped out on the railroads to the slaughterhouses in Chicago, the Texas beef was ultimately destined for the finely appointed tables of the east. Abilene upgraded its image as the original cow town mostly because of a famous native son, Dwight Eisenhower. The five-star general and future president of the United States grew up in Abilene, attended its public schools, and was returned to this city as his final resting place.

As dusk settled across the plains, I pulled off the interstate in Abilene and proceeded down Buckeye, across the tracks, and toward my childhood home on the outskirts of town in a journey back through time. When I stopped in the short driveway of a prairie-style brick house, I had peeled away my adopted facade of urbanity as if I had emerged unmolested from the clutch of Hades. I was anxious to see if I could belong again to the realm of simple things.

After stepping from the faintly smoke-scented rental car, I did not announce myself at first but instead walked the perimeter of the two or so acres that constituted my family's property. The small grove of Christmas trees we had planted behind the house when I was nine was in a state of bad repair. I could tell from the meager evidence of fresh stumps that there had been few, if any, sales transactions over the December selling season. My mind wandered back to past holidays when I had dashed madly around the property in my Santa Claus hat, hacking down evergreens and lashing them to car rooftops. Several of the heartier firs had grown well beyond the height that our small commercial enterprise could handle, lending an air of darkness and foreboding to the densely forested edge of our property. Directly behind the rear porch of our house was a small pond, fed by an underground source which we had never discovered. I was pleased to see that the pond looked healthy. A gibbous moon articulated crisply and defiantly against the surface of the water as I pondered my presence, reflected like a shadow on the surface of the water. I was ready to announce my arrival.

The outline of a discoloration on the bricks above the doorbell indicated the spot where a welcome plaque had once hung. Before I could ring the bell, the door swung open, and I was absorbed in a prolonged and jubilant maternal embrace.

The next few days have smudged in my memory. I remember the knot in my throat as I delivered nostalgic recollections to a sparsely attended memorial service for my teacher, Mr. Wertz. I spoke of the inspiration he had been to me, how he had provided the momentum that had accelerated my own personal journey. I described Wertz as an instrument of good, a man who had cared more about those around him than he cared for himself. And then I said that I would still plan to listen for the soft whispers of his advice, and that Wertz was surely watching the markets even as he had gone to a far better place. As I spoke, the image of Lucas Orr sprinted across my consciousness. I was angry at the intrusion.

When the service concluded, a small group of school-age children raised their voices in a high-pitched, angelic chorus. Afterward, perhaps a dozen of us stood around in the vestry, sipping tea and eating cookies. No one really knew what to say, and so very little was said. A woman I had never seen before approached me. Turning so she couldn't be heard by a bystander, she whispered a short thank you. Her bright lipstick and heavy makeup did little to mask the blemishes of advancing years.

"What you said about Bill was gracious and so heartfelt. Of course he was far from perfect as a man...he had his own demons. But I am touched that you remembered him so fondly."

"Well, thanks," I said. There wasn't much else to say.

"*If* he is up there somewhere, I know he would be smiling," she said. Momentarily disoriented by her strange comment, I had no idea what demons she was referring to. I had just delivered an emotional eulogy for Bull Wertz, but did I really know him? Did I really know anyone? I turned to ask the woman her name, but she was still talking.

"He was so proud of you, making it to Wall Street and all." She was masticating a green piece of chewing gum as she spoke. "That was really his dream for himself. He just wanted so badly to prove himself on the big stage, but of course he never really got the right opening. And then he took to the gambling—so sad. That proved to be a very poor substitute for his dreams, you know." I was realizing as she rambled how little I actually did know, after all. I wasn't even sure if she was telling me that Mr. Wertz was gambling on the stock market, betting on horse races, or playing high-stakes poker. She stopped speaking. "The ponies," she added, answering the question I hadn't asked. "That's what did him in." And before I could answer her, she patted my arm, turned, and walked away.

I remember a few other things about my return to Abilene. I can recall the evening whistle of the locomotives pulling out of town on the Union Pacific line. And I can still see the streetscapes of a world in which people walk slowly but stand straight. Before I left to return to New York, I had begun to feel more in control of my own destiny, at least enough to go to work on resolving the riddle which had come to possess me.

Among the earliest and most crucial skills I learned in my formative phase at Tantalus was the art of information extraction. Just as the shooter relies on the accurate sighting of his high-powered rifle, Lucas Orr taught the power of the telephone for a hunter of information. The premise was simple: a properly choreographed telephone call to a total stranger could elicit a valuable trove of useful and privileged information. I picked up the telephone in my mother's den and dialed the Social Security Administration office in Kansas City. A tuba-toned woman answered the phone at the main switchboard.

"Could I please be connected to the regional commissioner's office?" I asked. My call was transferred to a new location, where I was greeted by a somewhat more chipper voice.

"Ah, yes, this is Tim Paul down here in the Wichita office." The combination of short male first names would prove difficult for the woman on the other end to remember. "I hate to bother you with this, but I am new in the office, and we seem to have misplaced our directory. I have been asked to send a package up to the commissioner, and I just want to make sure that I have spelled his name properly. Could you help with that?"

"Certainly, the name is spelled D-A-G-G-E-T-T, Daggett. George Daggett," she responded quickly and unsuspectingly.

"That's great," I said, in a tone just short of profuse thanks. "I want to make sure that I get off on the right foot here. And what was your name, again, ma'am?" I inquired.

"Um-hum. This is Myrna; I'm Mr. Daggett's assistant."

"Thank you, Myrna," I said, and I signed off.

I made my second phone call to a different regional office of the Social Security Administration. Again I was able to obtain such relatively innocuous information as the precise titles of certain forms and the procedures and documentation requirements for filings—standard information that no one would suspect would be useful for anything more than filling out forms. These setup information-gathering calls were called "the probe," and they were essential to ascertain the proper terminology, so I could assume the air of an authoritative insider. Now I was ready for "the extraction."

For this crucial final phone interrogation, I had picked a small town Social Security office, ironically, in Manhattan, Kansas, where I assumed the staff would be less guarded and less likely to question authority.

"Good morning," I barked with an impatient air of someone in charge. "This is Dan Carl with Regional Commissioner Daggett's office. I'm calling because Commissioner Daggett has a family friend whose husband is recently deceased…widow will be coming in to your office later today to file the survivor's benefits. The commissioner wants to be sure this goes smoothly and has asked me to confirm the information you have on file for SS-5 of the deceased. Let me read you the social..." I offered up a crucial series of numbers that I had unearthed from the scrambled sheaf of old documents that Leonard Colesmith had given me.

"Uh, well, oh..." the kindly voice was wavering. "Usually we deal with..."

"I know that you usually deal with Myrna," I interrupted, "but we are jammed today, and the commissioner wants this matter taken care of immediately." That did the trick.

"Oh, yes, now what was the information you needed, Mr., er...?"

"The name is Carl. And what the commissioner needs for his friend is to confirm the original name registered on the SS-5, date, and place of birth for the social security number I just gave you." And then I added for good measure, "The commissioner also wants to know number of customers served yesterday in the Manhattan office and total sick days in the office this month." The art of extraction required that important questions be interspersed with trivial ones. Later, the interviewee would have greater difficulty recalling what the caller was looking for, if asked. Most often, they would only remember the final questions.

My now pliant Social Security staffer was pulling up a treasure trove of facts from the massive social security database, which would access and extract information nationally even though my inquiry had been entered though a small portal in a Kansas branch office.

"Okay, now I see a Lucas Orwin here, born September 20, 1951, in Sherwood, Pennsylvania. And then...here...we served thirty-six customers yesterday, and...what was that...oh yes, sick days. We are at twelve for the month to date. Was there anything else, Mr. uhh...er...Kerr?"

My demeanor now shifted, channeling warmth. "Now you all don't let that flu spread any wider. The commissioner can't allow the Manhattan office not to pull its weight," I said in a teasing tone. I signed off pleasantly, certain to be quickly forgotten.

Alone with myself again, I was delighted with the results of my sleuthing. Lucas Orr was really a Lucas Orwin of Pennsylvania. This mysterious mentor was now shape-shifting in front of me. Yet even knowing his original name, he remained hopelessly ill-defined.

With my missions accomplished—a final farewell to the memory of Mr. Wertz, a visit to my mother, and a series of calls from a phone that would never be traced—I took leave of my refuge, thrust back into chaos.

❧

When I arrived in New York, I was surprised to find Patrick waiting at the wheel of a black sedan resting curbside in front of my apartment.

"Get in," he said curtly. Soon we were racing down the West Side Highway, careening around other vehicles in Patrick's favorite high-speed game of chicken. He pulled onto a pier that projected out into the Hudson River and stopped, waiting for me to get out. I sat, awaiting instructions.

"Luc took the liberty of asking your friend, Miss Rocca, to join the trip. Your ride is waiting," he said, pointing a thick finger that sprouted small tufts of black hair. His target was a helicopter that sat on an active helipad.

It seemed to me then that Lucas Orr had taken absolute control of my life. On his command, I was about to enter a helicopter for the first time, traveling to an unknown destination in the company of a woman I was increasingly certain I had lost and who was mutating from my most intimate friend into a stranger. Patrick got out of the car, came around to the back door, opened it, and gestured for me to get out.

Dana smiled at me absently—as though I was someone she had met but couldn't quite remember—as I settled into the second-row seat of the sleek, black flying machine. She was anchored into her seat with double belt straps on both sides, making her appear immobile. A single pilot leaned around from the cockpit and motioned toward my seatbelt. I dutifully strapped myself down, and with a loud whirring noise and a sudden sideways thrust, we were airborne over the water.

For several minutes Dana and I sat without speaking, contemplating the shrinking landscape beneath us. Flying south along the river, we had panoramic views over the crush of civilization that sprinted across the New Jersey countryside, ending in the jumbled heap of a jagged border at the water's edge. I could see that Dana was scrutinizing the small streets of Hoboken out of her window. There was a longing and sadness in the way she kept her gaze fixed on the land.

We flew over the water until we cleared the lower tip of Manhattan and entered upper New York Bay. Magnificent views of the Statue of Liberty gave way to vistas of cluttered, crane-filled shipping terminals and Staten Island's sprawling Fresh Kills garbage dump before we were back over land, flying deep into New Jersey. After we had followed the serpentine trail of the turnpike for some time, I managed to breathe out a few words.

"Dana, what's your connection to Luc Orr?" I finally asked.

She turned to face me slowly and deliberately. I briefly remembered what she had looked like when she was happy, but now her expression was bitter and hard.

She didn't answer directly. Instead, she said, "Why would you ask, Nate? Didn't you send Luc to me?"

"No, never." Her glare was slicing into me. "What makes you think that? I mentioned you maybe once, but I didn't even think he was listening."

Dana wasn't convinced. She went on, "Wasn't that your plan...to tell him just enough to find me without giving away too much?" I replayed a series of blurred memories and jumbled conversations. I pondered the fateful moment on Luc's terrace after the night with Jasmin, when I had been unfaithful to Dana. I had guiltily told Luc about the woman I loved, and I added that she had put us onto the first deal I ever brought him. Had that been the trigger for Orr's recruitment? Or had he chosen her well in advance of my confession, just as he had poached me, deliberately and methodically? I had never imagined that Luc would involve Dana in his ploys. It didn't matter how it happened; there was nothing I could say to persuade Dana that I hadn't set her up. Orr had sacrificed me.

The landscape beneath us had become more rural, offering proof that parts of New Jersey were still entitled to be known as the Garden State. Panoramic stretches of farmland were occasionally violated by orderly arrangements of housing tracts. I could imagine a long-time farmer selling out when he couldn't afford the taxes on his land anymore. Perhaps he had experienced a couple of bad years, or maybe he needed the money to send his kids to college. Or maybe he just didn't care about the land enough to preserve it when he could have the money instead. The same thing was happening to farmland near the cities in Kansas. Suddenly the pilot turned sharply to the west, and we veered away from the turnpike. A few minutes—but many miles—later, we flew over an imposing chateau-style mansion and set down on a helipad adjacent to a broad, green lawn.

As the helicopter blades ceased their churning, and we could hear each other without shouting, Dana said, "Listen. We're in this together. Let's make the best of it." She grabbed my hand, squeezed, and let go as we descended. I had the impression that she had been here before, and it made me instantly uneasy. As we walked toward the house, a familiar shape in a handsome gray hat strode confidently toward us.

Orr spoke the first words, a curiously formal, "Welcome to Blackwell Manor." He grasped my hand firmly and then turned toward Dana.

"And it is so nice to see you again, Ms. Rocca," Orr said, looking at her an instant too long before turning back to face me. "I apologize for surprising you, Nate. I took the liberty of making Dana's acquaintance in the process of educating myself on the science of semiconductors."

"I see," was all I could manage to say.

Orr was at war with Quotient Corporation, and he had made Dana his useful ally. There was no place for moral ambiguity when Orr was engorged with the passion of conquest; he needed her, and he would have her. He did not pause to hear if I had anything more to say, and he turned to lead us towards the house.

"Please," he said, pointing toward the massive brick house as he touched Dana's shoulder softly with his other hand. I walked silently behind. A stone pathway led us through an arboretum of specimen trees before it emerged onto a lush, open lawn, centered by a large reflecting pool and a three-tiered fountain. Blackwell Manor was as spectacular in its own way as Luc's Manhattan triplex.

Orr assumed the hospitable air of a country gentleman offering refuge to a pair of weary travelers who had stumbled into his domain. Dana and I were shown to adjoining well-appointed guest rooms. While Dana retired to her bathroom, I sampled a tray of fresh berries. I stood for several minutes surveying the view from my broad window, which overlooked the rear of the property. A stone wall bounded the immediate perimeter of the lawn. Beyond, several acres of open fields gave way to brush and then to dense woods, where the trees were budding with the pale green sprouts of a new season. A swirling gray sky splotched with puffs of white rested heavily over the trees. When Dana came out of the bathroom and walked through the door that connected our rooms, her face was flushed and her eyes showed the evidence of tears. I wasn't prepared for that; she had never shown that kind of vulnerability before. I stepped forward to embrace her, and she went limp for a moment; then she straightened and pulled away.

We quickly recovered from our lonely, private moment and started downstairs, wandering through a maze of richly ornamented rooms. Walking through one of the grand salons, I let my fingers roll across the keys of a grand piano, stirring a small mist of dust and the awkward lament of a discordant tune. We found Orr standing at the side of an oval swimming pool that projected from the far-left rear wing of the residence. His back was turned toward us as he stared into the wind-whipped trees I had recently been surveying. A train whistle bellowed faintly in the distance.

"Ah, there you are," Orr said curtly, eyeing his watch. "We need to be on our way."

"You lead, I follow," I said, stunned into obedience.

Orr led us around to the front of the house, where a black Suburban was parked in a circular driveway. There was a thick-set chauffeur in a plaid cap and leather jacket occupying the driver's seat. Orr settled into the passenger's seat and gestured for Dana and me to sit in the back. The car proceeded down a long, curving driveway through an open field before dissecting a narrow allée of trees and then a tight hedge of arbor vitae that bordered the road side of the property. We exited through an electronic gate that opened and closed automatically as the vehicle turned onto an empty, two-lane country road.

We navigated a landscape of pasture and farm stands and modest homes set back from the road before turning into a gravel driveway. A simple wood sign read, "Welcome to Yeni."

"Yeni? What does that mean," I asked.

"It translates to mean fresh, as in 'new,'" Orr stated in curt response.

A series of smaller buildings set far back on the property were obscured from the road, and five or six yellow school vans were neatly aligned at the side of the buildings. Dana and I followed Orr into one of the boxy, two-story structures. He moved with intent and authority down a quiet hallway before opening the door and striding into a classroom of young children who were working at small tables on various crafts projects. A dozen curious brown and black faces turned to see who had arrived in their midst. A kindly looking older man who had been wandering from group to group stood to attention on Orr's entry.

"Mr. Lucas," shrieked a girl with a high-pitched voice and hair coiffed in a series of beaded ponytails. She rushed to Orr and hugged his leg in a tight embrace.

In a second classroom, where the children were engrossed in what appeared to be a series of small science projects, Orr elicited the same joyous response. We proceeded through a series of similar exhibits before heading outside where we found a small group of children studiously observing the edge of a small stream that flowed through the property, where they appeared to be involved in some sort of science lesson.

"No less than thirteen miles down the road lies one of America's most impoverished and dysfunctional cities. It is a crumbling place without hope, where drug-addled teenagers are thrust into the failing role of mother and nurturer, where toddlers spend lonely hours staring blankly at television screens, and where nature is thought of as something strange and far away," Orr said. He was showing us his shadow humanity.

"In this place, we practice defiance. We interject hope into young lives before bright eyes and smiles have disintegrated into hollow, desperate scowls or expressionless faces."

"This is a noble enterprise," I said, looking Orr directly in the face, which was shimmering bright white and reflecting direct sunlight as the brim of his fedora cast shadows back over his shoulders like a cape.

Turning to face me, Orr delivered his coup-de-grace. "It is only because I have emerged victorious in the fray of crass commercialism that these latent, noble impulses have been converted into something of substance."

The kindly gentleman from the first classroom had been lingering on the periphery of our conversation. Approaching me as Orr turned to leave, he motioned to attract my attention, his earnest eyes pouched with the wrinkles of experience. He looked at me seriously and said, "Lucas is a great and generous man."

As we drove away from Orr's personal laboratory of hope, he turned to speak to me from the front seat. "We have one other stop to make." Country roads gave way to streetscapes of homes with columned porches and gabled roofs. After proceeding down a quaint main street of boutiques, office storefronts, and sidewalks thronged with a sea of youth, we pulled up in front of two massive, eagle-crowned columns that anchored heavy, wrought iron gates. Through the gates a long path led to an imposing stone building.

"I am really not feeling too well," Dana said before the doors opened. "I think I am going to skip this part of the tour and have the car take me back to the house to rest." She hardly needed a tour of the campus where she had spent four years. I suspected that she didn't want to be reminded of the girl who graduated with high hopes and ideals, the girl who believed that working at a firm with the reputation Platt Brothers had maintained for so long would almost be like being a student at Princeton.

"Are you sure?" I instinctively reached a hand forward to touch her.

"That would be best," Orr nodded. "The car will return to pick us up." We stood together at the curbside, watching the Suburban disappear into a bustle of street traffic. As soon as Dana left, Orr was back on message, addressing me with the steady and confident tone of a college tour guide.

"Welcome to Princeton University, America's temple of higher learning. The building in front of you, Nassau Hall, once comprised all of the functions of the College of New Jersey, a school originally chartered to train young men as the ornaments of the state and the church. From those humble beginnings, this educational institution is now a beacon of scholarship and opportunity for men and women of all means, not only in this country but from all over the globe."

Pausing in front of two large stone lions, aged to green, that served as bookends to the seven steps leading under the arched doorway of Nassau Hall, Orr turned again to face me.

"And do you know what had to happen, before a magnificent yet fragile idea could ripen into the almighty and compelling institution we know today?"

I waited, knowing that Orr intended to answer his own question.

"The generosity of charitable men funded these buildings, these professorships, these scholarships. Men like Moses

Taylor Pyne, sharp-elbowed financier, steel magnate—and philanthropist. Or Henry Clay Frick, coal baron and strike-breaker, once known as the most hated man in America."

I followed Orr down one of the paths that crisscrossed a landscape of architectural splendor. Proud stone buildings were softened by climbing vines that had once been mere sprigs planted by an earlier generation of graduates. We walked by twin Greek Revival temples, home to legendary and secretive eating clubs, before pausing in an open space between a stone library that looked like a fortress and a soaring Gothic chapel.

"The land we stand on was a gift to the university from one of its most generous benefactors, a man whose fortune was built on the opium trade. This gentleman, whose reputation is now thoroughly cleansed by virtue of his final years devoted to civic and charitable endeavors, spent his most productive early commercial career in the begrimed pursuit of international trading and smuggling of a most noxious narcotic." Orr paused before delivering his philosophical finish.

"You see, Nate, it is never as simple as a schoolboy ethics lesson. There is no loathsome, and there is no laudable."

We turned to continue our tour along the pathways of the campus, passing a random assortment of coeds shuttling their backpacks between classes. Orr studied this flow of humanity with a thoughtful scrutiny that seemed to strike deep into a fleshy core of uncertain scruples. Several students turned to acknowledge his gaze as they passed, revealing a look of startled recognition. It seemed that more people recognized him by sight on the Princeton campus than on Wall Street.

After proceeding beyond a series of magnificent brick and stone buildings, we arrived at a super-modern structure skinned in a reddish-orange metal that might have been a postmodern play on the bricks of the other buildings, but it looked garish to me. I imagined the building's architect had spared no expense in its construction. Here we found our black Suburban waiting. As the door shut behind me, I looked up and saw that the name on the building was Orr Laboratory.

When we pulled back through the gate of Blackwell Manor, the final twinkles of daylight were finding shelter in the low horizon of western sky. Orr announced a time when we would all reconvene for dinner and then disappeared into his private quarters above a central staircase. Back in our guest suite, the door to Dana's room was open, but when I looked in I saw that she was asleep on her bed, curled in a fetal position. I didn't want to disturb her, so I went back outdoors.

I walked slowly, following a series of walking trails that had been carved through the estate's meadows, trying to think as the light of a cool evening waned. I felt like a creature lost in a maze of moral ambiguity. In a stretch of open field, I happened upon a pack of turkey vultures tugging the final shreds of flesh from a small animal that lay dismembered in the strands of tall grass. I instinctively looked away before I could determine which helpless creature had been taken down. Turning my face to the sky, I caught a glimpse of clouds illuminated against the silhouette of the moon.

When the shadows of night had rendered the trails impassible, I returned to the house, wandering through its formal first-floor rooms. I came to a large room guarded by a sturdy door with a formidable lock, but the door was ajar, and I entered a long room with no windows. The entire perimeter of the room was ringed with shelves lit by small spotlights, illuminating hundreds of gold and silver pocket watches. With a feeling that combined guilt and pleasure, I lifted a gold, open-face watch that sat beside a small inscription that read, "*G.P. Reed, Boston, 1871*" before picking up an equally impressive gold timepiece with a card that read, "*A. Lange & Sohne, Glashutte, 1882.*"

A voice behind me intruded upon my admiring exploration of this extraordinary collection. "A few more steps and you shall come face-to-face with the prize possession of the world's finest collection of antique pocket watches," Luc said proudly.

With a flourish, he walked past me and carefully cradled a gold pocket watch with a white enamel dial and bold Roman numerals.

"Waltham Watch Company, property of President Abraham Lincoln," he announced. "The president had it on him the night he was shot." Something about my reaction indicated to Orr that I was not sufficiently impressed with his extensive collection.

"Understand—this is not merely about the frivolous stockpiling of collectibles. Timepieces are history. The advent of a modern economy required synchronization. Railroad shipments had to operate on a schedule that could be understood by shippers and customers alike. Soon, the single town clock in a central square was supplanted by pocket watches that might be carried individually. But that status symbol soon became an entitlement of the masses. Progress."

I was struck by this unique chink in Orr's personality, a nostalgic connection to the past in a man who thought only about the future.

"Aside from their history, what is it about clocks and watches that fascinates you?"

Orr paused for a moment, amused by the question. "Clocks represent a delightful paradox. On the one hand, there is the certainty. The time is the time. But then, the passage of time is one of life's unfathomable mysteries. With every tick and chime, you have a little less time left in your life—and you never know how much less."

The ringing of a small bell cut the tour short. Dinner was served.

Orr's dining room was dominated by a long Chippendale table with six beautifully carved matching chairs on each side and an armchair at either end. Dana was already seated. She did not look up as Orr assumed his position at the head of the table while I took the seat across from her.

Orr rubbed his hands together as he addressed us. "I am truly grateful that we can be together for some rest and reflection. We are close to the culmination of something bold and life-inspiring. The time draws near."

I blinked apprehensively, and Dana said nothing.

For the balance of the dinner, Orr regaled us with a colorful history of American capitalism, heavily spiced with tales of the swaggering, bulbous-nosed financier J. Pierpont Morgan. According to Orr, when Morgan ruled the financial world, one of the few transatlantic phone lines then in existence was held open at all times exclusively for his use. Thus, breaking financial and political news was usually first to arrive at the House of Morgan.

"No financier has ever operated with a comparable information advantage," Orr said regretfully. "And no financier ever will again."

"But you come close?" I asked.

Luc replied without hesitating, "As the infamous cattle drover turned stock promoter Daniel Drew said when finally cast out by his sordid Gilded Age cronies, *'To speculate on Wall Street when you are not an insider is like buying cows by candlelight.'*"

The storytelling continued after the dishes had been cleared. Dana had remained quiet but observant during the evening, barely eating and holding a hand above her wine glass as the butler repeatedly replenished our goblets. Orr was telling a story about the blizzard of 1888, when I began to feel woozy.

"So Morgan had established a tradition of handing out Indian Head gold dollars to reward attendance at every one of the firm's partners' meetings, and the coins reserved for partners who did not attend were divided amongst those who were at the table. So then this great white hurricane hits New York unexpectedly in March, burying the city in two feet of snow while furious winds whipped up snowdrifts that rose to ten or fifteen feet or higher in certain places. The weather was so perilous during the two-day storm that the city's entire transit systems were shut down, and many stretches of roadway were completely impassable, even on foot." I could see Orr eying me indirectly.

"Wouldn't you believe it, the day the storm ended was the one day in the firm's history when every Morgan partner managed to show up for the regularly scheduled meeting, each of the greedy bastards fully expecting to claim a fistful of gold from his absent brethren!"

Orr's airy laugh reverberated painfully in my foggy consciousness, and I stumbled to excuse myself. I left him and Dana still at the table as I lurched and wobbled back to my bedroom. I collapsed onto my bed and passed out.

When I awoke, the somberness of deep night still enveloped me, while a splitting headache and a lingering stupor made me temporarily confused as to where I was. After fumbling to turn on a bedside lamp, I remembered that I was a visitor at Lucas Orr's great estate. I got up and opened the door to Dana's room and saw that she was not there and that her bed had been turned down by the staff, but it hadn't been slept in. A sudden outrage propelled me out of the room, and in the waffle-weave cotton bathrobe considerately supplied for guests, I wandered the dimly lit corridors of a very still house.

My purposeful roaming led me up the central staircase, where I had seen Orr retire earlier during the day. I paused to deliberate at the top of the stairs; a nearly full moon shone through the large triple window framed above the entry foyer. The door on my right was closed. But the door on my left was wide open, and through the haze of darkness I could see the flashing colored light of computer monitors. I walked into the room as quietly as I could and was relieved that the wide floor planks that looked as though they were hundreds of years old didn't creak. Once inside, I closed the door behind me and switched on the nearest table lamp.

The sudden flash was momentarily blinding, and I quickly removed the robe and flung it over the lamp to muffle the light. In the shadowed glow, the outlines of a large office revealed themselves. One long wall of the room was anchored by a broad desk covered with four computer monitors softly flashing green and yellow symbols. A neat row of large Rolodexes sat beside the technology array. The opposite wall was covered by a floor-to-ceiling bookshelf, filled with financial history books and the biographies of famous financiers.

Tong, tong, tong. The sonorous incantation of a clock somewhere in the house momentarily startled me, and I was afraid it might arouse Luc or one of the staff, and I would be discovered. I barely breathed, but when the house remained silent, I gathered my composure and resumed my intrusive exploration. As I looked up, I saw something singular and remarkable on an upper shelf. It was a photograph, an object I had never seen before among the vast personal possessions of Lucas Orr. While his private collections included such vintage images as a Robert E. Lee daguerreotype and an original photograph of Amelia Earhart before her final expedition, this was something else entirely.

The scene showed a boy of perhaps ten with a girl several years older hugging him from behind. The girl was exceptionally pretty, with wavy fair hair and a big smile, but there was an unfocused quality about her eyes that created a sense that something about her wasn't fully tuned in. A magnificent, alert German shepherd sat next to them, as though on guard. The dog's chest bulged, with a large blond patch that shone like strands of gold as it reflected the light. The dog's large snout was a deep black. The ears stood upright, pert, and serious.

The boy was a miniature version of my youthful-looking boss. Without hesitating, I removed the photograph from its frame, and in my larcenous mood, I surveyed the room for other items that might serve my purpose. My attention was drawn to the series of Rolodexes, and as I thumbed through them quickly, I noticed that most of the cards held the names of companies, some familiar to me, and others not. I shuffled to the letter "Q," and there I found what I wanted, a card that read, "Quotient," with a phone number, but no name, scribbled below the entry.

After extinguishing the light and retrieving my robe, I quietly slipped back into the hallway. My senses tingled in alarm when I saw a dim sliver of light I had not previously noticed in the crack at the bottom of the facing doorway. I scampered down the staircase on my toes, listening for the fateful sound of a door opening behind me, but all was still. After concealing the heist in the travel bag I still had from my trip to Kansas, I pulled a thick cashmere blanket around me and listened to the rhythmic pulsing of my heart.

The patter of rainfall was the first sound I heard when I awoke. Sitting up in bed, I saw Dana perched in an armchair ten feet away, watching me closely.

"You slept soundly, I gather?" her question was posed seemingly without an underlying meaning, and I held my tongue and gathered my faculties.

"The weather will prevent us from flying. There's a car waiting downstairs to drive us back to New York," Dana said. She was leaning forward uncomfortably in the chair as she spoke.

Scrambling out of bed, I piled into my day-old clothes and picked up my travel bag. We found Orr downstairs in the main foyer near the front door, where he rose to meet us.

"I trust you had a restful night?" he asked.

Swallowing the tidal wave of hostility rising within me, I managed to force out a meek reply.

"Sure...yes...it was fine," I said, and I wheeled, anxious to be on my way, but Orr interceded.

"Nate!" I turned to face Orr. The violence of his delivery made the hairs on my neck stand up. "I need you prepared for the week ahead. The climax is upon us."

I nodded submissively, hoping that his hard scrutiny would not reveal that I was beginning to feel my own power rising. And then, in a semi-sprint, I was heading for the car; Dana followed more slowly.

The clapping of windshield wipers was nearly the only sound in the car, except when the storm's winds blew against the rain. Dana and I barely spoke, although as we made our way along the turnpike, with trucks splashing water in great bursts against the car windows, I asked haltingly if she wanted to talk.

"No," she said. "What's done is done, Nate. Perhaps each of us...if we were stronger..."

"But maybe this is making us stronger..." I said, trying to muster an argument.

"Perhaps...if we had made different choices at small forks in the road along the way...but now..." She shook her head, and her voice trailed off. What was there to say? Dana had spent the night with Luc Orr; I had spent part of the night raiding his office. We were no longer the people we had been when we thought we were in love with each other—and with Wall Street.

I wanted to plead, to persuade her that we could return to the way things used to be, but I knew she was right. We had irretrievably forsaken each other. I caught the driver looking at us in the rearview mirror before he turned quickly away.

Hoboken was our first stop, and Dana opened the door. She was out of the car before I could say anything, and she walked away without looking back. I knew it would be futile to follow her.

When the driver dropped me in front of my apartment, I waited for him to drive off, and then I turned away from my front door and set off on a new mission. I was in a race against time, and my opponent was a man who did not lose.

CHAPTER ELEVEN

As the Vanderbilt fortune soared, the Commodore's mental faculties began to deteriorate. He spoke of erecting a 625-foot obelisk in Central Park to celebrate himself and the nation's first president. Perhaps, in his own mind, this was also meant to serve as a memorial to the president's namesake, his own dead son, George Washington Vanderbilt. He increasingly sought the company of clairvoyants and spiritual healers who might help him commune with spirits from the afterlife, including famous deceased financiers, his son, and his mother. He also developed a special relationship with a fetching young practitioner of "medicinal magnetism," a woman fifty years his junior who soon took up residence in his Washington Place townhouse. Meanwhile, Vanderbilt's second wife—who also happened to be his first cousin twice removed and who had been wed to the Commodore when he was the ripe old age of seventy-seven—was usually safely exiled across the river in the family mansion on Staten Island while the Commodore frolicked. Some strange new force had evidently become resident in the tycoon's brain.

∽

I held my breath as I swiped a magnetized card across the key plate for access to the Tantalus offices and exhaled when I heard the reassuring click. The place was empty, as it typically was on most Sunday afternoons. I knew the office would be buzzing with activity by nightfall, however, as the analytical team prepped the game plan for battle that arrived when the bell sounded on a new business week. But for a while, I would be able to work in solitude.

I opened my travel bag and, shuffling though a pile of soiled clothes, removed the purloined photograph. I studied the details of the scene and the facial expressions closely before setting the picture aside. This would have to wait. Then, removing the Rolodex card I had pilfered from Orr's home office, I nervously dialed a California phone number. An answering machine picked up on the first ring.

"You have reached the Wink residence, and we cannot presently take your call. Please leave a message, and we shall ring you back."

I hurried to the Tantalus file room, a lonely, well-lit space where the firm housed the deal files for every one of its investments, past or present. A separate access card was required for entry to the low-ceilinged windowless room, which was tightly packed with row upon row of steel storage cabinets. A large, industrial-sized shredder sat in one corner, its blades prepared to grind furiously at a moment's notice. As I stood on the threshold of this vault of knowledge and power, I contemplated the secrets and stories that resided here, shackled in torment and locked away. How many weak-willed businessmen had been intimidated or blackmailed? How many careers ruined? How many innocents lost? The ruminations heightened my anxiety and hastened my task.

A quick search of the neatly organized archives provided the answer to my central quest. Stuart Wink had served as the chief technical officer of Quotient Corporation when the company had first gone public. Within a year, he had sold his entire stockholding in the company and announced his retirement. The press release announcing his replacement, a senior executive from another well-respected tech company, had been replete with thanks and praise to Wink for a job well done. The reason given for his departure was the standard, "for personal reasons."

That was precisely the professional profile I had expected to find behind the source of Orr's startling Quotient Corporation discovery: a senior person on the technical side of the business who had privileged access to the troubling database documenting medical afflictions. The fact that Wink had left the company so quickly after it became a public entity, and thus subject to considerable exposure, only made me more certain of my discovery. I now had a name to associate with the angry, bathrobe-clad retiree who had passed the dangerous dossier to me at the Waldorf Astoria.

"Very sorry, Stuart," I muttered to myself. "Your life is about to get a little complicated when the SEC comes calling."

I hurriedly sped about the balance of my preparations. When I had finished typing out a letter exposing Orr's plot against Quotient Corporation using the pilfered company data, I carefully removed a neatly folded single sheet of Quotient property from my wallet. The page was titled in bold letters, "Quotient Corporation: Worker Health History Summary." I had copied this solitary piece of evidence from my Waldorf dossier before handing it off to Orr. I placed it, along with my anonymous communiqué, in a large manila envelope, which

I addressed with anxious dispatch. In large, block letters, I wrote the address for the SEC's Division of Enforcement in Washington, DC.

I had one more task to complete. Entering Orr's office, I dropped the childhood photograph on his bare desk. The intent of my message was clear: I know who you are. As I turned to leave, a sudden bolt of sunshine streamed through the partition where a single blind had been stuck open and slightly askew, temporarily startling me. I stepped out of the glare as the offending stream of light crashed into the opposite wall. I was feeling Orr's presence. I took a final look around the place that had served as my dungeon of indecency for nearly a year and then rushed out, down the elevator and onto the street.

I walked for a dozen blocks, cutting back in my tracks several times as if to elude some trailing surveillance, before deciding upon a mailbox standing sentry in front of a convenience chain store. I held the potent package tightly over the gaping mouth of the mailbox for several long seconds before releasing a torrent of accumulated regret into the chute, along with the envelope. The postal repository clanged shut with the swiftness of an executioner's blade.

I returned to my apartment, feeling the exhilaration of a man sprung from captivity. The impatient jangling of a telephone was audible even before I entered into my spartanly furnished abode. I picked up the phone and heard Orr's voice, speaking in a barely controlled hiss.

"You have taken something that belongs to me, Nate." He had probably been trying to reach me for hours. Thoughts of family pictures and file rooms and Hoboken, New Jersey, swept through my mind.

"And you have taken something of great value from me as well, Luc," I said steadily, although the fury I felt surprised me. Orr remained speechless for so long that I was aware that he was still on the line only because I could hear the faint sound of air being inhaled.

"Stay where you are. We can work this all out. I am coming to see you," Orr said, bundling his emotion back in check. I hung up without responding.

No sooner had I returned the phone to its cradle than its shrill clangor startled me anew.

"Don't bother; it's too late," I blurted out.

"Oh, there you are; I just wanted to tell you that you left a red notebook here in your bedroom. It looks like it might be important work material, and I just didn't want you to worry about misplacing it. Shall I send it?" My mother's voice was momentarily disorienting, given my manic frame of mind.

"That won't be necessary, Mother. I'll be back to get it."

"Okay, dear, a mother must check. I love you, Nate." My mother's perky fidelity could be annoying at times. The phone call was concluded almost as soon as it began. Midwestern frugality had no place for gossipy, long-distance phone conversations.

Knowing now that I had little time to waste, I quickly dialed Dana's apartment, hoping that she would answer. I wanted to cry out a warning, to plead with her, to offer my support, but instead of the expected answering machine—or Dana herself—I heard a disconnected number message. Armed with the clarity of open conflict, but simultaneously hindered by the uncertainties of my mysterious foe, I fled my apartment for safer ground.

I spent the night in a forty-dollar room at a bedraggled boutique hotel on the Upper West Side, where I paid in cash. The tiny room had cable television, my only requirement. Late into the night I stared into the crazed, crossed eyes of Jack Nicholson, who was raging around in an isolated, snowy resort. When the movie was over, I lay in darkness, listening to the ticking second hand of a clock on my bedside table. Unmolested by competing sounds, the ticking grew louder and more oppressive. Something in the maddening regularity of that infernal beat suggested chaos and not order. I thought about Orr's theory about the paradox of clocks.

When I awoke, streams of a new day illuminated random flecks of dust floating in the air above me. I stared up at two tiny strands that jousted with each other before coupling momentarily and then breaking apart. Jumping out of bed, I hastily dressed in clothes that were by now several days old. Then I worked myself up to a heightened state of alertness at a neighborhood coffee shop before returning to my hidden lair, which looked filthy under the glare of sunshine. After putting the chain on the door, I turned on the television again. All I could do now was wait, a helpless eyewitness to a cheerless scene.

The familiar floating globe of the Financial News Network was displayed beside the large, white letters, FNN. At the bottom of the screen, a scrolling ticker of white and blue indicated the stock prices of America's corporate icons.

"What a silly business," I thought to myself. "Imagine spending a lifetime speculating on the random wiggles of chance."

I sat entranced by the simple ciphers that indicated ups and downs, success and failure. As the markets opened for trading, the numbers sprang to life, and I watched fortunes rise and fall across the bottom of a television screen. A news anchor interrupted my stupefaction with a recitation of the morning's business news before my attention returned to the dancing digits. I sat listlessly, but alert, waiting for a sign of the end.

Suddenly, I sat bolt upright as the four letters Q-T-N-T, indicating the stock ticker for Quotient Corporation, rolled across the screen, with a stock price next to the symbol. There was a brief pause while the familiar and unthreatening HD of Home Depot and the MCD of McDonald's scrolled by in turn. And then those fateful four letters recurred, and the price was five dollars lower than the first print. And then again and again, those letters rolled by, indicating that the shares of Quotient

Corporation were trading very actively at falling prices that morning.

A beaming, heavily made-up face, the eyelashes thick with mascara, was now centered on my screen. In breathless revelation, this financial reporter's job was to convert breaking financial news into entertainment, and she did her job superbly.

"The shares of Quotient Corporation are plunging in early trading, and here is what we have been able to confirm so far. A research analyst issued a very downbeat note this morning, describing a massive potential liability that the company may face as a result of unreported hazards in their manufacturing process. And get this—the report was issued by Platt Brothers, the very same firm that is leading a billion-dollar underwriting for Quotient that was expected to price as early as Tuesday. This is a stunning turn of events that has shareholders in a blind, selling panic…"

Picking up the bedside telephone, I slowly dialed seven familiar numbers after hearing the scratchy buzz of an outside line. Tom McGuire picked up on the third ring, an unexpected delay that gave some hint of the chaos that would greet me on the other end of the wire.

"Mac, it's Perkins. What happened?" I could barely hear my own voice over the strains of pandemonium flowing into my earpiece.

"Perkins? Perk!" McGuire suddenly lowered his voice to a hoarse whisper. "Perk, I thought I had seen it all, but this one really takes the cake."

"What, what is it?" I blurted out.

"So, you might have heard that we are running this Quotient deal, a nice chance to ring the cash register for the Brothers Platt. The seals were really barking for this one—the book was three or four times oversubscribed." McGuire paused to inhale.

"And...?" I was bursting with impatience.

"So today the syndicate department announces at the morning meeting that the deal is being accelerated to price tonight, the demand was so overwhelming. The sales force is itching for the meeting to end so they can bang out a few last calls to fast-money accounts who like to play the hot deals—you know the drill, right, Perk?" McGuire was relishing drawing out the story in the face of my impatience.

"Please, just—what happened?" I was pleading now.

"Out of nowhere, Dana Rocca—I expect you remember that hot piece of ass," McGuire hissed. Even in a crisis he couldn't resist making a crude remark. I was holding my breath as he continued.

"Well, she walks into the room, and she has this stone-cold zombie stare on her face. Then she hands out two stacks of research notes and climbs to the podium. Cullman is running the meeting, and he obviously is not expecting her to speak, because he looks stunned when she grabs the microphone. We are all expecting some rah-rah, over-the-top final push on the

Quotient deal. But she stares at us blankly for about a minute and then simply says that she has uncovered new insight that makes it impossible for her to support the offering. She is cool as a cucumber, I am telling you, Perk, as she describes a load of damning medical data that is now circulating through the room on Xerox handouts. And then she finishes by saying it would be irresponsible for the offering to go forward until the company comes clean about their liabilities." McGuire was nearly hysterical at this point.

"Then she stands up, apologizes, and walks from the room. And then—I am telling you—all hell breaks loose." McGuire gasped for breath again and grew silent as I heard mumbled voices in the background.

"The lawyers are crawling all over this place, Perk, telling salesmen to call clients and disavow the report, saying that it was not properly reviewed, blah-blah. As if they can put the genie back in the bottle on some legal technicality. And they are trying to find Dana to get her to come back on the hoot and retract her comments, but she is gone. They found her office completely cleaned out. Hey, Perk, you think this mess might clip my bonus? Perk?" The jabbering voice of Tom McGuire faded out as I laid the receiver back down.

After months of meticulous planning and seduction, the collapse in the share price of Quotient represented the brilliant culmination of Orr's plot. Undoubtedly he had revealed his damaging findings regarding Quotient to Dana just before the deal closed, leaving a choice between two paths, both of which led to her destruction. Either thwart Orr by subverting the truth and forsaking her own ethical code, or publicly disclose Quotient's dark secrets, destroying the company and her own career while enriching Lucas Orr in the process. In the end, Dana had stayed true to herself as Orr, no doubt, had expected.

I picked up the phone again to make one more call. The voice of Duncan Bridges was upbeat, as I expected it to be.

"Nate, it's great to hear from you again. Have you thought about that proposal of mine—to come down from your dark perch and work with me? It's a little less prosperous perhaps, but plenty of psychic income here at Bridges Capital."

"Have you seen the stock price of Quotient this morning?" I asked bluntly. There was a sound of clicks on a keyboard, followed by an audible gasp.

"That's us—that's me. I am not sure what I have done." I paused before blurting out a question. "Duncan, are there any truly good people—unequivocally good people—on Wall Street?"

Duncan Bridges did not hesitate in his response. "Of course there are. There are plenty of people with integrity, people in the business whom I trust completely. But good people can also make unsavory choices. I've seen firsthand that the sirens of Wall Street can magnify ordinary human foibles. The temptation of money—big money—is powerful, and the path to great success can sometimes force choices that lure you into the shadows." I was beginning to think, or at least to hope, that Bridges was one of the rare people who lived under the disinfectant of constant daylight.

"Thanks, I appreciate your helping me put this in perspective. Perhaps I can stop by to see you again," I said. My confessional completed, I rang off and turned back to the scrolling ticker on the bottom of the television screen.

The moneyed insiders of Crouse & Potter had sustained a loss stretching into the billions of dollars. But beyond the monetary ramifications of Orr's assault was the visible damage to reputation that could prove even more dangerous. CP would need to strike back quickly and savagely to stamp out the injurious opponent before their large financial setback led to a presumption of sustained vulnerability. In the financial business, you were either winning or you were losing. There was no comfortable resting place for players in repose.

What the partners and lawyers of Crouse & Potter did not yet know as they planned their formidable retaliatory response, an assault that would eventually center on Lucas Orr and his Tantalus Fund, was that I had already launched the well-trained arrow to strike down their foe. I should have felt the surge of excitement aroused by the exercise of power, but I did not. Neither did I feel the sharp throbbing of personal responsibility. I was numb and merely going through the motions. I was a minor actor in the background, awaiting the climactic scene of a destructive drama.

CHAPTER TWELVE

The evening before Commodore Vanderbilt died, he was moved from the bedroom in his Washington Place home, where he had been confined to bed rest for nearly eight months. Raised upright in an adjoining sitting room with a view out to the snowfall of a gathering blizzard, he had conversed excitedly with family and friends well into the night. For that one evening, the once keen mind of the unrepentant tycoon was animated again, offering no evidence of the wasting fabric of a failing body. His cheeks and eye sockets were hollowed to an inert gray. His calves had shrunk to a circumference half the size of a healthy man. Large and inflamed bedsores dug into the sagging flesh of his right hip and thighbone. Deposits of congested tissue clogged the right ventricle of his heart, his liver had been wasted by atrophy, and his colon was ulcerated in several places. Medical journals would later reveal that the deterioration of his inner organs was owing to advanced stages of syphilis.

His eyes twinkled as he reflected on the millions plundered from the corner of the Harlem stock and moistened as he relived his early days on the Hudson, hands on the tiller of a small sailing vessel. To hear the Commodore's mumbled musings was to apprehend the perfect harmony of an unscrupulous gatherer of money, thrust upon a nation's commercial landscape. The wrinkled, dying man confessed that a mania possessed him; it was the pursuit of moneymaking.

In the deepest hour between midnight and dawn, a sharp turn toward death occurred. The Commodore had suddenly grown much weaker as his condition became rapidly worse. Shortly after sunrise, the immediate family was summoned to the bedside of the distressed marauder, wasted and now too frail to utter a word. Vanderbilt's valet, an elderly black man, was called upon to sing a religious hymn, which he delivered in a beautiful, deep timbre that brilliantly melded the sorrow and the majesty of the moment. Then Vanderbilt passed from this world. Later that day the massive glass roof of the train shed at Grand Central Depot would collapse under the weight of snow.

∽

Safely removed from the hubbub of New York and in no particular haste, I spent several days wandering the back roads of the Pennsylvania countryside in a rented car. I lingered in the parks and small shops of unmotivated towns like Elysburg, Milroy, and Grampian, where the coffee was poured slowly and where a New York license plate might prove to be a lively topic of conversation. Like a hunter wearily approaching his prey, I moved slowly but methodically toward my destination, guided by three simple clues: a name, a place, and a photograph.

I finally arrived at Sherwood, a town only a few traffic lights removed from the interstate and a place that seemed conflicted by its identity. It struck me as a burg that might have been birthed somewhere out in the landlocked middle of the country, that at a young age had gathered itself up with purpose and crawled across the continent for the coast. At some point, too tired to travel another step, Sherwood had abandoned its journey and merely plopped itself down, smack-dab in the middle of Pennsylvania.

I encountered my first phone booth on a stretch of sidewalk shared by two contrasting merchants who eloquently expressed the town's mixed heritage: Grissom's Hardware and Lumber and Lucy's New York Boutique. Leafing anxiously through the list of names neatly arrayed in thin, white pages, I arrived quickly at the listing that I was seeking. Tucked between "Orvos, James" and "Osborne, John" was an entry that simply read, "Orwin, E." I fumbled nervously for some spare change to deposit into the narrow coin slots and dialed the phone number. The phone rang four times before it was answered.

"Hello," the response was shallow, soft, and sweet.

"Ah, yes. I am calling—excuse me, good morning, ma'am." I struggled to find the right approach, knowing that what I said next would determine whether a mystery would continue to haunt me.

"Mrs. Orwin, this is Nathaniel Perkins, a friend of Lucas'. I am in town. Could I...could I...drive over to see you?" My fate was suspended in an interlude of still air for an awkward eternity. Finally, I heard a throat being cleared, and the voice spoke simple directions in a deeper, subdued tone.

The plain, two-story, white frame house was set back on a lonesome property whose front lawn had been freshly mowed. Behind the house a small, detached garage appeared to have a living space above. The sweeping, broad canopy of an oak tree pressed up close to the house, obscuring the view from the second-floor windows, which faced out toward open fields. A covered porch shielded the front door, which opened before I had a chance to knock. Lucas' mother surveyed me with a look that was neither hostile nor distrusting.

I introduced myself, and then I said, "I know about Lucas Orwin. Can we talk?" A spark of life briefly flickered in her eyes. She motioned me inside before I had a chance to speak.

"It has been so long since I have heard that name…so long since they all left me." She walked toward me as she spoke.

"Thank you for seeing me," I offered weakly.

She offered her hand. "Emma Orwin." The grip was soft. She slowly mounted a narrow central staircase, motioning for me to follow. She turned the knob of a room at the top of the carpeted landing, and we crossed the threshold into a chamber that held the dreams of a young boy. The exterior foliage shadowed the room, preventing much natural light from entering through double windows facing the front yard. There were books and school pictures, some medals hanging from a mirror, and a large stuffed dog that might have been the carnival prize at the county fair on a steamy summer night. But, although it was crammed with the bounty of a youngster's enthusiasm, the place was lifeless.

"This was Lucas' room until he was twelve, and then, afterwards, he moved out into the apartment above the garage. He said he needed to change."

"Afterwards…?" I asked.

She turned abruptly, the tour apparently concluded, and I followed her back down the stairs to the main foyer, where she took a seat in a well-worn chair with a view to the road, and she motioned for me to sit on a bench opposite her.

"Lucas would have been a teacher, I am sure, just like his father up at the university. He was a good man. And Lucas, so observant as a child, just absorbing all of the details of life, and with such a spark, such a passion."

As Mrs. Orr seemed to drift deeper into an ancient memory, I was afraid that my chance was fading. I interrupted before she could escape into the wrong part of the past.

There were three living beings in my purloined photograph, the only physical evidence in my possession. I took a wild stab at getting to the core of the story.

"Did something happen to his sister?" I asked, visualizing the image of the pretty, smiling girl in the photo, so full of life as she hugged her younger brother, but with something unfocused in her eyes.

Mrs. Orwin's eyelids fluttered, and I could see tears welling up.

"Do you have any siblings, Nathaniel?" she asked. I thought briefly of saying I did, but I decided that honesty would be the better approach.

"Unfortunately, I am an only child."

"Maybe when you have children of your own you will understand the hurt of parenting. You do the best you can under the circumstances you have—but fate always gets the final word..." She was starting to drift again, and I needed to pull her back. My question about Luc's sister hadn't evoked an answer, so I tried again.

"Why does your son despise dogs, Mrs. Orwin? I know that he had a German shepherd as a boy."

"Despise dogs? Lucas loved that dog. And, oh, did Queenie love that boy. They would spend hours together exploring all manner of places."

"But why...?"

Mrs. Orr went on, speaking more sharply now.

"Queenie was devoted to Lucas and to April. That dog could be very protective—maybe too protective..." I leaned forward and took Mrs. Orwin's trembling hands in mine.

"April was, well, you know, what these days they might call 'slow'—though some of the words that were used about her in those days were a trifle harsher. It would make Lucas so angry—he protected his sister, and he trained Queenie to protect her, too." The narrative was flowing quickly now, and I held her hands even tighter.

"Well, Lucas and Queenie were returning home from one of their walk-arounds when they happened upon April with the postman in some bushes behind the house." Mrs. Orwin was crying, but she continued to talk.

"She was resisting as well as she knew how, but this distasteful human being was attempting to have his way with her—she was so pretty, and so innocent. This wasn't the first time a man had tried to take advantage of her, but before it had always been boys in school, and Lucas took care that they knew never to bother her again. The poor, sweet girl really didn't understand..." Mrs. Orwin's chest was heaving as the story tumbled out of her, and she was trembling so badly I was afraid she would be unable to go on.

"Lucas didn't hesitate; he set Queenie on that vile and lecherous creature, and Queenie did her job. That scum was in the hospital for six weeks, and he went blind in one eye."

"What happened to the dog?" I asked, afraid that I already knew the answer.

"There was an investigation. Of course, the postman denied everything. They accused April of being retarded, said she led boys on, didn't have control of her faculties. In the end, they ordered Queenie to be destroyed."

"How awful!" I said as my mind spun with anger and sympathy.

"Lucas was outraged. He talked about how unfair it was that the righteous were forced to suffer while the wicked went unpunished. When they came to take Queenie away, she and

Lucas were gone. Lucas took her for a last rabbit hunt in the woods behind our house. He brought his shotgun and a shovel, and the two of them set off as though they were going off for an afternoon of fun. It wasn't long before I heard the shot. Hours later, Lucas came back alone. He was never the same after that."

Mrs. Orwin released her hands from mine, wiped her eyes, and leaned back in her chair.

"My son was right about one thing—the world is not fair," she said.

"After that, April began to have more trouble with men. Our family doctor said the only way to protect her from her natural impulses, which would surely lead to her getting pregnant—it was just a matter of time, he said—was for her to have an operation that would make it so she wouldn't want a man. He told me there was a doctor, Walter Freeman—I will never forget that man—who performed something I later learned was called an 'ice-pick lobotomy.'

"This Dr. Freeman was so smooth, so convincing. He described an enlightened approach for treating mental patients, basically taking certain of their feelings away by performing a special operation that was supposed to cut off some part of the brain so the patient would be calmer. Only afterwards did I learn that the operation basically involved poking a pair of ice picks into the brain through the back of the eyes."

"Jeez!" I breathed. I remembered reading that President Kennedy's sister, Rosemary, had the same kind of lobotomy when she was in her early twenties, and it had destroyed her mind.

"I agreed that April could have the operation; I thought it would make it easier for her. Maybe it worked, but that depends on what you mean by working. She was such a happy child, and even as a teenager when the troubles started, she was cheerful. But after Dr. Freeman got finished with her, she was no more than a blob of a person. I couldn't keep her at home, and we finally had to put her in a public institution for the insane. That poor girl wasn't any more insane than I am.

"That's when Luc decided on his quest. He wanted to make a lot of money, control his own destiny, and take care of his sister. Now he's bought her a nice little house and pays for people who live with her and care for her around the clock. She even has a little dog, one that won't bite anyone. She carries it around like a baby.

"Lucas never forgave me for letting that doctor operate on his sister. As soon as he could, he left here, got himself a scholarship to State U, and that was the last I saw or heard from him. Before he left, he told me he would never come back. I won't ever forget the look on his face when he said that he did not want to be reminded of a time when he believed the world was good and fair."

Sadly, she added, "He does continue to watch over me. Long ago he set up a trust for me, so I would never be in want."

I was so horrified by Emma Orwin's story that I told her a little about Luc and his success, explaining it from his point of view, describing him as a man who cleaned up dirty companies. I asked her for a glass of cold water, and then, as quickly as I could without hurting her feelings, I got back in my car and sped away from that melancholy place. The source of Lucas Orr's sometimes senseless cruelty, his obsession, and his drive had emerged from its dark void. A life lived according to half-truths was now illuminated by a new and softer light. My quest was over, and I felt a desperate need to see him again. I rushed back to New York, weighed down by an apprehension that I would not arrive in time.

On my return trip, I stuck to the quicker approach of the major interstates, concrete boulevards that had long since banished broad swaths of the bucolic backwoods from the view of hurried travelers. Shortly after I had entered the reception area for a New York all-news radio station, I heard the self-important voice of a deep-throated newscaster blaring away the headlines while the familiar sound of teletype clacked away in the background. Something about the inanity of that voice made me stop. I pulled the car off the highway at the next exit. And there, with my face buried in my hands, I finally unleashed the torrent of muzzled emotion that Orr had taught me to restrain at all cost. Around me the traffic of an ambivalent civilization surged on ahead, undaunted and undeterred.

CHAPTER THIRTEEN

A sturdy, six-story brick structure on the corner of Broadway and Twenty-second Street has been transformed over the generations, posturing interchangeably as dwelling place, saloon, and office building. But in the early days of April of 1882, the place was known as the Glenham Hotel, a somewhat downscale version of the swank Hoffman House just up Fifth Avenue. The neighborhood was bustling, alive with the energy of a city on the move and on the make. After the Civil War, Madison Square Park, across Fifth from the Hoffman House, had become one of New York's most prestigious addresses when the city had marched ineluctably northward. Retail shops, churches, and expensive hostelries glowed with the favor of civilization's elite.

The slender man with a close-cropped brown beard who paced in room seventy-nine on the fifth floor of the Glenham Hotel on that April day was deeply troubled. His wan, hollowed complexion and stooped frame gave evidence that he was in poor health. He was a singular sort of individual, the kind of person who always seemed on the outs with everybody. The son of a famous father, he had tried hard to live up to the expectations of his namesake. Shipping off to California without his father's approval, he had staked his claim to greatness when gold fever had seized the land. But he had not proved strong enough to survive the coarseness of life on the Gold Coast. Physically infirm and professionally unaccomplished, he had become brooding, dissatisfied, and petulant. Then the seductive lure of the gambling tables had taken their hold, and the ensuing toll of debts only further alienated his demanding father. When the tycoon died, in a crushing final

227

affront, the son had been deprived of any material inheritance. The father had left only the income from a small trust for the son, to protect him against the destructive consequences of his own rashness.

Cornelius Jeremiah Vanderbilt, the discarded son of America's richest man, sat on the bed of his rented room at the Glenham Hotel, put a revolver to his head, and pulled the trigger. The bullet landed just four inches from the exit wound, resting softly on the pillow.

ᕮᕤ

When I arrived back in New York, I quickly discovered that my attempt to right the Tantalus wrongdoing had achieved dramatic results. I was astonished to learn that Ashton Malpas was dead. I was somewhat less surprised when I found that Lucas Orr had disappeared. In the aftermath of the Quotient affair, the offices of the Tantalus Fund had been raided by the FBI. Subpoenas had been issued to all current and former employees, with the firm facing multiple counts of insider trading and securities fraud. Crouse & Potter and their allies in the financial press were hollering for retribution, but a dissection and analysis by the nation's financial regulators would take years to unfold, given the tightly-controlled manner in which the firm had been run, the dearth of record keeping, and—most importantly—the absence of either of the firm's principals.

In the end, a myriad of complex charges would be alleged against Tantalus over a period stretching back over many years. But delivering justice would be another matter. A substantial portion of the firm's capital had vanished, dissipated into a dense thicket of offshore trusts and untraceable bank accounts.

Malpas, as the chief operating officer and head of compliance, knew that withering scrutiny and a long jail term awaited him. There was only one escape. He had descended the stairs to the subway station and stepped in front of a speeding express train heading downtown on the number five line.

When the authorities arrived to examine Orr's office, the place resembled a bare classroom during the summer holidays. The window blinds had all been raised, and a flood of spring sunshine streamed in to illuminate every corner of the cavernous suite. But there was nothing to see. The shelves and drawers were empty, and the neatly arranged desk merely held a computer monitor, a phone, and a blank pad of paper.

Dana had resurfaced to sit for an interview with the investigators, a fact that I discovered during multiple aggressive questionings, to which I had also submitted. The authorities pressed hard to widen the net of felonious actors beyond Orr and Malpas. But they had been frustrated in their attempt to accuse anyone beyond the principals with either a clear motive of personal financial gain or a willing and informed complicity in the activities of the Tantalus Fund. Lucas Orr's stealth and complete control of the operation had provided a perfect alibi for Dana and me. In the end, we had both been branded as tools, stagehands—not actors, directors, or authors. My penalty would prove to be a mere résumé blemish, a professional association that would repel some prospective employers while intriguing others. Dana, I later heard, had sought refuge in the cloisters of a leafy Connecticut suburb, where she took a position at a small independent research boutique.

༄

Dampness clung to me as I entered the house of worship, a humble, low-profile edifice tucked into a midblock side street off Times Square. It was the kind of structure that you might walk by every day for ten years without ever glancing up to notice its simple gray magnificence. The church owed its existence to the generosity of one of New York's early magnates, who stipulated that it was to remain forever a "free church," meaning that parishioners would not have to pay pew rents.

The stone gaze of the Virgin Mary eyed me sadly as I retreated from the neighborhood of blinking lights and bustling commerce. Inside, the building unveiled its beauty, but the sanctuary was silent and nearly empty. Along the right side there were several smaller chapels. In the far corner, behind the main altar, a simple room was adorned with a high, vaulted ceiling, painted with murals of the Epiphany. A marble statue of the blessed mother hung above a simple altar that was bracketed by two tall candles that flickered with the golden blush of a tentative flame. I took a seat, alone, in the holy room.

The minister standing quietly in front of the altar smiled at me and nodded. Behind him were three soaring stained glass windows. A simple table had been placed in the center aisle, and a cross of heather and roses had been carefully placed on its surface. The minister discreetly eyed his watch and waited.

Two elderly women who had been shuffling through the church paused in the doorway. After whispering to each other, they too entered the chapel and took a seat. I wondered who they were and whether they were just passing by, or were there to pay final respects to the secretive Ashton Malpas. As we waited, the space remained still, lifeless, and expectant. Choirs did not sing. There was no harp, no organ, and no trumpet, only the silence at the center of the dismal void of death. It appeared that we would remain alone and that the celebration of the life of a man who had once been very wealthy would be a pitiful and lonely affair.

"I know that words cannot gild this grief." The priest's delivery roared forth as if he were attempting to be heard above the clamor of a thronging audience in a vast hall.

"In the common bed of death, the mighty and the meek, the worthy and the unworthy alike all lie side by side." The words touched a memory point in my brain, and I recalled a stanza from a favorite poem that I had memorized as a young boy:

> *The saint, who enjoyed the communion of Heaven,*
> *The sinner, who dared to remain unforgiven,*
> *The wise and the foolish, the guilty and just,*
> *Have quietly mingled their bones in the dust.*

"And why should they fear the judgment of the afterlife, for the stains of this world cannot enter through heaven's celestial gate!" The booming eloquence of the words seemed out of place in this nearly empty room.

As I looked around the spare space, I stopped hearing the words, even while the orator's lips moved and he motioned his hands meaningfully. A single crucifix hung on a wall to the side of the altar. Separated from the crucifix by a brightly lit wall sconce was a carving that depicted the death of an elderly man, probably a saint. He was surrounded by a tightly packed group of men whose faces carried the heavy look of despair. But he gazed upward, welcoming a promise of eternal life. My own gaze remained fixed, hypnotically, on the scene until my dark reverie was interrupted by a pleasant-smelling presence that sidled up quietly next to me.

"Hello, Nate." I recognized the voice instantly.

"I hope I'm not too late," she whispered softly in my ear. I smiled as she gently squeezed my hand.

"Hello, Jasmin."

The two women turned to survey my new companion, and when I looked at them, I saw that one more spectator had arrived and was standing partly obscured in the entry to the small chapel. It was Ted Newman. He and I looked at each other, and he slowly nodded his salutation. He had the strange and knowing look of a director overseeing a final dress rehearsal. I turned again to face the minister, who was concluding his remarks as he walked slowly back to the altar. Then, deliberately and methodically, he held a snuffer over the candle flames. First one and then the other emerged from under the suffocating canopy in a brief burst of dancing, angry black smoke.

"Luc was the candle, and you were the snuffer," Jasmin stated without any hint of animosity or recrimination. It was true.

"I wish I could talk to him once more. I know things now that I didn't understand," I offered meekly in response.

Suddenly I recaptured a memory. It was a strange twist to the Tantalus myth. It was alleged that Tantalus had stolen a golden dog that had been assigned to protect the infant Zeus. But when he was confronted, Tantalus denied any knowledge of the heist. He was a liar and a larcenist, but he also represented mankind's hopeful, yet futile, grasp for the rare and valuable, even when it could never truly be his. I was drifting in a dream, desperate to finish a lost conversation with Lucas Orr. I wanted to go back to the moment on his terrace when he spoke to me, with vulnerability, of dogs. I recognized at last that Luc had been speaking of longing and loss.

"Don't say it, Nate," Jasmin whispered, startling me back to alertness. "If he was here, if he could speak to you, he would not judge you or even resent you. This chapter of your life— and of his—is gone. Don't even look back."

The minister stepped down and disappeared through a side door, and the ladies left too, but Jasmin and I sat in silence a little longer. A glance back toward the empty doorway revealed that Newman had not waited for the service to end. I was relieved, not knowing what we might be able to say to each other.

After a few silent minutes when each of us was alone with our thoughts, I took Jasmin's hand and we stood to leave. Under the circumstances, it would have been appropriate if a fine, drizzling rain had been falling as we exited the church, but we were greeted instead by ribbons of sunshine poking through a late April sky.

"I will be going now," she said. I struggled in vain for the right words, something that might help to fill the void that was enveloping me.

"Time heals the pain," was the expression that came out. It was what everyone said, but it was true.

Jasmin smiled and then entered a waiting taxi and glanced back once to look at me as she faded from view. When the vehicle rounded the corner onto Sixth Avenue, I spun in the opposite direction, scraping the shine from my fine new leather wingtip as I turned.

As I ambled away, I wasn't thinking about the lonely Ashton Malpas, whose body was probably already on its way to some desolate domicile, but about Lucas Orr. I was certain that he would never be found. His brief, brilliant, and delusional reign atop the citadels of finance would soon become just another episode in New York's forgotten lore. But I could never forget him, the captain of a ship that had capsized in a violent storm. Unable to rescue himself, he had clung frantically to the bodies that surrounded him, slowly dragging them under. Briefly in his clutches, I had lost my livelihood, my love, and my innocence. But I inhaled deeply, tasting the old air of a bustling city as I savored my good fortune.